Bad at Love

Gabriela Martins

UNDERLINED

This is a work of fiction. Names, characters, places, and incidents either are the product of the author's imagination or are used fictitiously. Any resemblance to actual persons, living or dead, events, or locales is entirely coincidental.

 Published in the United States by Underlined, an imprint of Random House Children's Books, a division of Penguin Random House LLC, New York.

Underlined is a registered trademark and the colophon is a trademark of Penguin Random House LLC.

Visit us on the Web! GetUnderlined.com

Educators and librarians, for a variety of teaching tools, visit us at RHTeachersLibrarians.com

Library of Congress Cataloging-in-Publication Data is available upon request.
ISBN 978-0-593-48344-2 (trade pbk.) — ISBN 978-0-593-48345-9 (ebook)

The text of this book is set in 11.75-point Baskerville MT Pro.
Interior design by Jen Valero

Printed in the United States of America
1st Printing
First Edition

To everyone who ever worried
their English wasn't good enough

Author's Note

The idea for this book started with Daniel—a fake bad boy. I wanted to write about what it was like to have everyone assume you're something you're not, and not have the confidence to speak up against it. Sasha came later, as a force of opposition with her own agenda, a girl hardened by experience and the life she's had. In many ways, I feel like we all have some Daniel and some Sasha in us. Part of us that is terrified we're not good enough to be where we've earned to be, and part that reacts defensively just in case that fear is true. This is a story about two teenagers finding themselves and love, but also about making peace with our inner Daniels and Sashas.

We've earned this. We deserve to be here. We can breathe out in peace.

1

Daniel

These sunglasses were a major mistake.

My agent, Bobbi, gave me the shades so I don't squint at the paparazzi flashes. With them, no matter how harsh the lights, I'll still look good for the pictures. The downside? At night I can barely see an inch in front of my face.

To be clear, I didn't even want to go to this party. I would've loved to be in bed by ten. But my bandmates, Sam, Wade, and Penny, wanted to par-tay after our jam session, and my sister, Helena, insists that I *make friends.* So here I am, at midnight, hardly awake and stumbling my way out of the Blue-Bearded Man in LA, after spending three hours pretending to drink at the club.

We step onto the dirty sidewalk and into the hurricane that is the public eye.

Oh, paparazzi, how I have not missed you.

There's at least a dozen of them, plus a cluster of fans. Eight months after joining Mischief & Mayhem, I'm not surprised anymore when I see the M&M fans screaming and crying. Though it *is* weird when the fans scream, "Rotten! Oh my God, please take a selfie with me!"

That always takes me a moment. Oh. Yep. That's right. I'm not Daniel anymore.

I'm *Rotten*.

Luckily, we're shielded by security people as we make our way to our car, two tall people in black suits with earpieces and serious faces. The woman in front of me is named Yasmin. As I found out a few weeks ago in the green room at a radio interview, she can break-dance better than anyone else I know, but right now she's an impenetrable wall, and I love her all the more for it.

Yasmin and her partner clear the way for us, but there's still *some* impromptu press to be done. Sam's the best at it. I wish I had his smooth confidence. He's about my height, with thick longish hair mussed back, and colorful clothes. He has a triangular face with a strong jawline, light caramel eyes, and a ridiculously charming dimpled smile. Sam's so charismatic that even though he's just gotten in front of me, stopping a fan from getting a sort-of-not-really selfie, the girl only swoons at him instead of getting upset.

Sam's usually the fan favorite because he's ripped and has a million-dollar smile, but somehow I have my share of fans. People who, inexplicably, chose me as their favorite M&M band member—who think that without my addition to the band, we wouldn't be making the most anticipated album of the year.

They've got it wrong. I feel like I'm bullshitting my way through this, and anytime now, someone will find out. I'm most afraid it'll be Penny, since she's the only one in the band who seems to value my creative opinions.

A TMZ reporter, a woman with a high bun and a ferociously bright smile, elbows her way past the fans. "Mischief and Mayhem! How are we doing tonight?"

Sam greets her, while Penny and Wade take selfies with fans. Penny may lose the title of fan favorite to Sam or me, depending on who you ask, but she is definitely the press favorite. She's pretty and fun, with her colorful locs matching her nail polish, and her big brown eyes, just a shade darker than her dark Black skin. The reporter eyes me like a hawk, but I stay quiet. "Rotten, word on the street is that you stole Trent Nicholson's girlfriend. Is it true that you're seeing Reese Brown?"

Trent Nicholson? Reese Brown? Who are these people?

I turn to Sam for help, and he chuckles. "Oh, a gentleman doesn't kiss and tell. Do you really think Rotten would say anything, Martha?"

How does he know her name? We're all just seventeen. He can't possibly be *friends* with this woman. This whole interaction confuses me. I tuck my hands into the front pockets of my black skinny jeans, which is tough, considering how tight they are and how many rings I'm wearing. Scanning for the car, I spot someone dart past Yasmin. The girl is fast, and suddenly her phone is in my face, so close that I stumble back and fall spectacularly onto my butt.

All eyes turn to me. Cameras flash. That's all I needed—further "evidence" that I'm drunk, even though I'm completely sober.

Great. Absolutely great.

I lower my head, clearing my throat and pressing the shades against the bridge of my nose.

Act cool, Daniel. Here you're *Rotten.*

"Rotten?" Penny asks. Wade is behind him, thick black eyebrows raised in concern. I don't hear what Sam says, something to try to distract the reporter, Martha.

I'm picking myself up off the pavement, and Yasmin is escorting the fan back, when all hell breaks loose. I barely have time to brush the dirt off my hands before the fans seize the opportunity to break through our security line.

Security breached. *This is not a drill.*

A dozen fans with a wall of security people between you and them is nothing. It's easy-peasy. But a dozen people rushing straight toward you, with absolutely no barrier, feels like a million people. And you're prey.

My eyes widen as I backpedal.

This is not bragging. This is contextualizing my downfall: they don't come for Penny, Wade, or Sam, not at first. They *all* come at *me.* And so I run.

It's like I'm suddenly in a zombie movie. I'm wearing a neon-green floral shirt, and I'm acutely aware that the Los Angeles night is not dark enough to hide me.

Am I going to die if they catch me? I'd rather not find out.

Making my way around the building, I duck into an alley. A girl my age steps out of the club's side door, probably leaving the party we left too. She's wearing a mustard-colored dress and holding a big black leather jacket. Her long brunette bob frames her face, her nose is hooked, and her eyes are so dark that they seem black. They're the darkest eyes I've ever seen, and I want to look more closely.

I'm on a mission, though, so I ditch that thought. She's my potential shield.

Attempting a smile, I approach her. "Please save me," I beg, breathless.

She parts her lips; then her eyes flick over my shoulder and she notices the small crowd turning the corner to find me.

"Can I have your jacket?" I try again.

Her big round eyes stare up at me, but she doesn't protest when I close the distance between us and reach over to pluck the jacket out of her hands. I swing it over my shoulders to hide my screaming shirt.

She seems to register the panic in my eyes, because she takes charge, saying "Act natural" in a low voice and pulling me into a fake embrace—to hide me in plain sight.

Okay. Good plan.

Both of my hands awkwardly brace against the brick wall behind her. It's cold on my fingertips.

My adrenaline is still high, and my chest's going up and down from running, so I hold my breath, staring at her. I wish I weren't wearing these stupid sunglasses.

She's examining me, like she's trying to make up her mind about something. She frowns at first, studying me from head to toe but not pushing me away. Her jacket hangs from my shoulders, threatening to push both of us into darkness.

"Where did he go?" I hear a man ask from the sidewalk.

"Shoot, they're coming," I whisper.

"Shoot?" she echoes, cocking an eyebrow. "Shut up and don't look their way." Her warm hand touches the side of my face, directing me to look at her. Her lips are shaped like a heart.

I try to stand still.

Impatient, she rolls her eyes and pulls me closer by the front of the jacket. For a second I think she's actually going to kiss me, but then I realize that her big dark eyes are still open, staring at me, a cross between annoyed and curious.

Her forehead is an inch from mine. We're so close that I can feel her breath against my face.

She can't feel mine, because I'm not breathing.

The people passing us only see a couple making out in an alley. A guy in a black leather jacket and a girl in a mustard dress. Not a rock star on the run. So they keep going. The paparazzi, the fans. They all keep going, and we become wallpaper, part of the background, like the distant music pounding from the club.

And the thundering sound of my own heart.

She drops her hands and walks around me like it's nothing. "They're gone," she says.

I want to apologize for accosting her, but before I can,

she looks past me once again. I pivot and see Wade with a security guard shadow.

Wade is a lanky Korean guy, a little shorter than me and Sam, and twice as stylish. He's got bleached-white hair in a mess of curls, dark monolid eyes, a button nose, and a preference for all-black clothes. He's wearing an oversized sweater full of awkwardly placed holes, with black skinny jeans and black Converse.

"Hey there," he says, I suspect more to her than to me. He flashes her a smile.

She narrows her eyes.

"There you are." Penny comes after him, gesturing for me to unglue myself from the brick wall. "We thought we'd lost you. The car's waiting, and Yasmin's not happy about what happened."

I give them a curt nod.

Then I turn toward my savior, wanting to thank her—but I can't force the words out, for the same reason that I don't say anything in interviews. Will she even understand me through my Brazilian accent? It's so much thicker when I'm nervous.

I offer her my hand to shake instead, hoping my eyes say *Thank you.*

She gives me a weird look before taking my hand.

Hers is soft and warm. I can't help it—I smile.

The alley is illuminated by a flash, and I silently curse.

I never smile. Not on camera.

There's a paparazzo in front of us with a manic grin,

holding his camera like an award statue. After that, he runs. A breath later, Yasmin appears at my side, ushering me out of the alley and into the car. Before I know it, I'm in our black van, staring at my empty hand.

Sam and Wade flank me in the car, and Penny sits in the row in front of me, with Yasmin and her partner beside her. As the driver takes off, Sam turns to me and notes, "You weren't wearing this jacket before."

My eyes widen, and I take the girl's jacket off from around my shoulders. "Oh. Crap."

But Sam and Wade don't pay me much attention after that. They start debating about which hidden VIP room is best for taking girls to make out, while the closest I came to making out tonight was technically fake. It's like I don't even exist. Penny turns to join in, scolding them in a playful way. Always the three of them, plus me.

Penny, Wade, and Sam—high school friends and bandmates who have known each other forever. And I've only known them for eight months. It's like they never really see me. Not the real me, anyway.

Which is okay. I zone out, holding the leather jacket in my hands, looking at the strange pin of a coffee cup with a cloud drinking it, and think about its owner.

It's nothing, I tell myself. These butterflies in my stomach will go away. But the girl in the mustard dress stays with me the whole ride home.

2

Sasha

"What has the cereal ever done to you, Sasha?" Mom asks, with a hint of smile. She sits across from me at our small kitchen-living-room table.

I roll my eyes and turn my attention back to the cereal. I wasn't planning on telling Mom about what happened last night when I was ambushed by Rotten in that alley, but I'm not sure if I can hold in my frustration much longer.

"It's nothing," I try. "Work stuff."

"Don't speak with your mouth full." She checks her watch. "We have fifteen minutes before I have to leave to start my shift at the superstore. I'm not in cashier mode yet—I'm in mom mode. The sooner you start talking, the more time we have to come to a solution."

Groaning, I slouch in my chair. She stares at me, and my willpower crumbles. "Ugh, okay. I was chasing a band for LA Now. I actually convinced a security person to let me in through the back door, and then lost them once we were inside. And then, when I had an *actual* shot at getting a photo while they were leaving the club, I missed my chance."

"I saw that you got home really late." She gestures for me to give her the elastic around my wrist, that I mostly keep there for her, and then she pulls her hair into an effortless bun that makes her look even younger than she is. "I know it's just the beginning of summer and you're enjoying your curfew-less life, but you know that ends in August, right? It's going to be your last year of high school, and you'll need to stay focused on getting into college."

I love how she says this as if we have any money for college—as if my best bet after graduation isn't getting a full-time job at LA Now or another tabloid that will pay me for photography. Often I feel like Mom lives in her own world, a world in which we don't split most of the bills like roommates. A world in which she can pop champagne when my college acceptance letters roll in.

Instead of getting into it, I say, "But this is my job."

"It's an internship," she corrects me.

"Aaaanyway." I start again. "They were all there. Penny, Wade, Sam, and *Rotten*." I pause, letting the ridiculous nickname sink in. "Why's everyone so into him anyway? He's a skinny giant. At least Sam's, like, muscular or something."

It takes less than a second for recognition to flash in her eyes as she registers the names of the Mischief & Mayhem band members. I sort of hate that she knows exactly what band I'm talking about. Then again, she does love *Making*

Music!, the reality singing competition where the band initially formed.

"Sam's too nice," she explains, shrugging. "Rotten's cute, Sasha. Isn't that undercut or sidecut or whatever it's called trendy right now?"

"He's the worst," I deadpan.

Mom tilts her head to the side, like she finds this amusing. "It's not like you to have opinions about artists."

"What are you talking about? I have plenty of opinions."

"You don't have opinions on artists. You have opinions on their music. You usually don't care about who makes the music." The way she says it, I sink in my chair a little lower, because she's absolutely right. It's all about the music for me. "What's special about Rotten?"

I remember him last night, the way he was looking at me. . . . My face heats up.

And I stab at my cereal some more.

"Not special. Annoying," I correct her. "He parties too hard, he's always grouchy, and he hooks up with a different girl every week! Plus he thinks he's too good for the rest of the band."

It's like Mom hasn't even heard me. She notes, "Everyone loves bad boys."

She had me until she said that. Because, okay, Rotten's not, like, horrible-looking. And his undercut looks kind of good. His hair seems so soft, and when I touched his cheek in the alley, it was a little scruffy.

But then Mom goes and mentions *bad boys*. Her dreamy look is disgusting. I know who she's thinking of, and it's not the famous guitarist of the hottest band of the hour. "Sure. Everyone loves bad boys who knock up girls and then leave them behind. It's really cute."

It's Mom's turn to roll her eyes. "That's not what happened."

Yeah. I know, but still, close enough.

"I'm sorry. Dad *cheated* and then left."

While most Brazilian and Brazilian American mothers wouldn't let their daughters get away with saying things like that—or at least I would guess not, based on the horrified looks we get from other neighborhood parents when they overhear our conversations—it's different with us. Maybe it's because we're so close in age, my seventeen to her thirty-one. She has always been more of a best friend than a parent.

She dismisses my comment and circles back to last night. "Okay, okay. So Mischief and Mayhem showed up. What's the problem? Blurry pics? Couldn't sell them to Lloyd?" My chaotic boss at LA Now. I shake my head.

I'm not sure I should tell her that I missed my opportunity for a tabloid-worthy photo because I was pretending to make out with Rotten.

Having waitressed part-time at the celeb-friendly Angeles Diner every summer since freshman year, plus this recent tabloid gig, I'm not really ever starstruck. My only thought when I see a hot celebrity is that they never look as good in person as they do online. The shadows around their eyes are always a little deeper, their hair is often a day too dirty, and their tone of voice is seldom as nice as when they say "Hi, guys!" on Instagram Live. Seeing Rotten up close didn't shake me because he was famous. Seeing celebrities is normal for me.

It sort of shook me in other ways, though. Like how I still remember the feel of his shoulders under my fingertips. And how he smelled like soap. That caught me off guard.

"Rotten was wearing shades, so we couldn't see his eyes in the pictures. Probably as high as a kite." I gesture dismissively with my spoon, and my cereal spills. Mom glares at me, and I tone down the intensity. "Anyway, not only did I miss my opportunity for a good shot but someone else took a picture of him making a move on me."

"What?" Mom gasps.

"I mean, it was sort of fake, but yeah." I wrinkle my nose. "PopGloss already posted pictures of us together, calling me the 'Mysterious Girlfriend.' And now I have a message from Lloyd saying he wants to talk today." The thought of getting scooped infuriates me all over again. I saw Rotten first. I should be the one getting the exclusive. But you can't get the shot when you're part of it.

I don't know what I thought would happen when I covered for Rotten in the alley. Maybe after the pretend make-out ended, I'd demand an exclusive interview? I just . . . reacted. I wasn't thinking.

Mom grabs the cereal bowl in front of me and slurps down the milk. "I can't believe you're so ungrateful. This blessed boy is our ticket out of poverty."

She's joking, but I still sigh dramatically. "Yeah, I'd really score millions being his Thursday one-night stand."

Mom laughs. "All right, it's time for me to take my bus. What time is your shift at the diner today?"

"Only in the afternoon. But before I go there, I have to stop by LA Now and beg Lloyd not to fire me." I force a smile, and she smiles back.

"I'm sure you'll do great."

"Hey, Vanessa." I wave at the secretary as I enter the office. LA Now is an online magazine with half a dozen employees, and though the office is small, it's still downtown Los Angeles. From our windows I can see palm trees, shiny billboards, and Hollywood Hills off in the distance.

Vanessa blows a big bubble before replying. "Hey, Sasha."

I clear my throat. I'm sweating a bit. "Um, Lloyd called. He said he wanted to see me."

Vanessa flashes me her phone. It's that picture of Rotten and me, the one PopGloss posted. "It's probably about this." You can't see me clearly in it, just my blurry profile, but if you know me, I'm recognizable enough.

I don't say anything at first. Then I ask, just above a whisper, "Do you think I'm going to get fired?"

"You're not really hired, so you can't get fired," Vanessa says helpfully.

Um, thanks for the reminder. I lean against her desk and survey the office. Most of the employees are trust-fund kids that Lloyd knew in college, with the exception of Vanessa and Earl. Earl is the accountant, aged approximately a hundred and twenty years old.

Vanessa, on the other hand, went to the same high school as me, and I owe this internship to her. She was a senior when I was a freshman, and we both worked at the school newspaper. I suspect Lloyd only lets me take pics for them because he has an obvious crush on Vanessa. He never takes me seriously otherwise. He or anyone else here, for that matter.

"But I want to be hired. I want to work here," I tell her.

It's not actually my dream per se, but working here full-time after I'm done with senior year wouldn't be half-bad. At least I already know the people, and Vanessa likes me. I know that I can secure my place at LA Now if I keep delivering pictures . . . which I didn't do yesterday.

"Aim a little higher," Vanessa advises me, but she has an amused smile on her lips. She wheels herself forward, but her wheelchair bumps the corner of her desk. "And tell Lloyd that if he doesn't make this place more accessible, I'm suing him."

Even though I can't tell whether she's serious, with her lopsided grin, I nod, absolutely aware that I won't have the guts to say anything like that. Not until I'm a real employee. She gestures for me to go into his office, so I take a deep breath and knock on his door.

Lloyd opens the door with a manic smile.

"My favorite photography intern! Future reporter! Come in!" He spreads his arms, taking a step back. At only twenty-six, the CEO of LA Now has failed up a few times; his parents rented this place and gave him the funds to start the magazine just a few years ago. I only wish I could be that lucky.

I walk in slowly, half expecting there to be a camera capturing this prank. Lloyd is many things, but complimentary isn't one of them.

"Sit, sit," he says.

And then he actually *pulls out the chair* for me to sit across from him.

I take a seat and wait for the other shoe to drop. Because it's coming. This is a guy who took turns calling me "Natasha" and "Shelly" for the first month of my internship. There's no way he's going to be okay with a lowly intern fumbling exclusive photos.

"So last night . . . ," he starts, and then he looks at me, like he expects me to keep going.

Lloyd believes in dressing casually for work. He thinks he's a young Mark Zuckerberg in the making. His eyes are not just any shade of blue but an especially uncomfortable one, like a vampire's. I hate making direct eye contact with him, especially when he's staring so intently at me, as if he wants me to tell him all my secrets.

"I . . . yeah. I'm sorry I couldn't get any pictures of Rotten. . . ." I trail off.

"Before he fell in love."

"Yes." I nod. Then frown. "Wait, what?"

Lloyd smiles from ear to ear. It's a little terrifying. "You are our diamond in the rough, Sasha." Right name. Very suspicious. "I can't believe a high schooler is about to give me the scoop that's going to put LA Now on the map!" He clasps his hands together. "So are you on board?"

"Am I . . . ?" I look around. No cameras. "Lloyd, listen. I really don't have any idea what you're talking about."

"I saw the pictures and videos from last night. Rotten is really into you. If you agree to play along, there's a huge story here."

Laughter erupts from me before I can stop it. Rotten? Into *me*? He probably doesn't even remember me. Nope. Completely forgotten.

Lloyd's smile slips.

"I mean, I'd love to help," I say in a rush. "I would. But it wasn't like that. It was just a very awkward . . . I don't even know what to call it."

"You're not seeing the big picture. He's into you. Now you've got to pretend like you're taking the bait. Go on a few dates, record your conversations with him, get some photos—and bam! We've got a scoop."

I shift uncomfortably in my seat. "I mean . . . aren't there enough stories about this guy? He hooks up with someone different every weekend. I'm not sure there's a bigger headline than that."

Lloyd adjusts his hoodie. "That's where you're wrong, Sasha. These guys *always* have worse skeletons in the closet. All you have to do is open the door." The metaphor is creepy enough without his piercing vampire eyes, so I look away, trying to think of an excuse. He seems to sense that, because he adds, "Get us a good story, and I can offer you something worth your while."

My voice cracks a bit when I ask, "Are you going to let me write that story? Are you going to give me a byline?"

"Sure. But I have more interesting plans," he says. "Mom was telling me how we should start a program for people like you. You know?"

In my head, I try every label I can think of: Brazilian? Child of immigrants? Brown? Pansexual? High schooler? Photography aficionado? He must see that I'm trying to figure out what he means, because he explains.

"An inclusivity program, if you will." He winks.

I hold my breath. "What for?"

"A program that believes in voices like yours. A scholarship program. The application is due at the end of the summer. Maybe the financial aid could make a difference for your college plans?" He raises his eyebrows. "A twenty-thousand-dollar scholarship is nothing to sneeze at."

"Twent—?" I gasp.

"There are three people on the board, but I'm basically making this decision." He shrugs, glossing over the fact that the other two people are his mom and dad. "So tell me, Sasha. Are you in?"

So that's why he was smiling like a shark. Because he knows that I'm prey, and there's no way I can say no to an offer like that.

3

Daniel

We don't actually do any rehearsing in the thirty seconds we're left alone in the studio by our producer. It's easy to see why the band is called Mischief & Mayhem. Wade throws a massive paper ball at Sam, but it lands on Penny instead. She takes her water bottle and squeezes it in his direction. Wade screams as if he's been mortally wounded. Sam tackles him to cover his mouth and stop the screaming, but Wade bites his hand. Now it's Sam who's howling, while Penny snaps at both of them to shut up. All the while, the three of them are laughing.

I am watching a crochet tutorial with the sound off. It couldn't be more obvious that I don't belong here.

I have never really belonged in the band, even though I've been part of it ever since the producers of *Making Music!*, the reality singing show we all competed on, paired us together to compete as a band. Me, the lone guitarist from Brazil. Plus Penny, Wade, and Sam, three kids from an LA arts high school who had been trying to make it big. Penny on the vocals, Wade on the drums, Sam on the bass, and me on the lead guitar. *Making Music!* turned out to be a big break for all of us, but it's been a big adjustment too. It's been two months since the show finished airing, and now we have to wrap up our debut album by the end of the summer. I think we're all hoping to prove we're more than reality TV stars who barely fit together, but I'm still having trouble convincing myself.

When Silva, one of the album producers, arrives, he finds Wade soaked, Sam nursing his bitten hand, and Penny holding her water bottle behind her back. His pale face turns bright pink.

"Hi, Silva," Penny says, offering her coyest smile and sitting back down.

Silva takes in Wade's dripping hair and then spots the paper ball. "I—what?" His shoulders sag. "I don't . . . Okay. Whatever. I have some ideas for 'Ulterior Motive' that I'd like to run by you."

It's going to be only our second original single after being on *Making Music!* Our first single, "Generation Emancipation," was number one on *Billboard* for three weeks and is still hanging out on the charts.

Penny sits a little straighter, her eyes sharpening, and Wade and Sam get quiet immediately. "I like 'Ulterior Motive' the way it is. . . . I thought we were going to keep working on track eight? We still need a title for that song, by the way." She shoots Wade a look; he's mostly the one to come up with the titles and, often, all the lyrics.

"I know," Silva says, eyes on Penny, like she's the only one in the band. "But I had a different idea for the intro that I think might work." He pulls his chair closer to her and opens his laptop. Without warning, he plays the beginning of our song: my guitar shreds, and immediately Penny screams into the mic. "I was thinking we could have a start like a jingle here. You can play the keyboard too, right?"

I sort of like the song intro as is too. I feel agitated, my leg going up and down, but Silva doesn't look at any of us boys. Penny nods at his question, because of course she can play the keyboard as well as the acoustic guitar, bass, and ukulele.

"What if, to play with the idea of being fooled, we start with a ballad-like jingle, with you singing the chorus very softly, and *then* we have the guitar shred and everyone else comes in?"

Penny muses at this. She turns to Wade first, then to Sam.

Sam says, "I think it could work. Maybe not for the radio version, but it could be disruptive in a good way for the album version."

Nobody asks me, and I don't feel comfortable enough to speak up. Ever since our days paired together for *Making Music!* it's been hard for me to just say what I want, especially creatively. They were together before, and I was a last-minute addition to Mischief & Mayhem.

It barely feels like I'm part of the band now, and it's been eight months. When is it going to start feeling like it?

"I just wish we hadn't cut 'Inconsequence.'"

They all look at me, and I freeze with the guitar on my lap.

Oh. Shoot. Did I say that out loud?

Penny blinks, Sam cocks an eyebrow, and Wade looks like he's never seen me speak before, which is a bit much. He notes, "You didn't say anything last week when we agreed to cut it."

My shoulders tense and I feel sick. Still, I clear my throat, trying to shrug away the feeling that I should shut up already.

"Well. Nobody asked me. So."

It was the one song I had a hand in shaping. Penny and I spent three weeks composing that song together just after we finished the reality show in second place. She thought that we'd been robbed, since our fan base was the biggest and we'd improved the most as a band over the course of the show. I was just annoyed at everything. The winner had been this tall white guy with blond hair and a constantly mean expression. It had felt like a waste of time, all of it. Leaving Brazil and my parents behind, making my sister babysit me in the United States, working so hard to speak English more confidently.

Penny composed most of the lyrics, but I wrote most of the melody. And then we filled in the blanks for each other. It wasn't only that "Inconsequence" meant a lot to me because of the timing. It was my first composition *ever.* The first song that would feature my name as a writer.

But Penny didn't seem to mind it getting cut. She had her name on most of the songs. I didn't say anything. It just stayed on my mind, enough that the words tumbled their way out of my mouth before I could stop them, and now my bandmates are all looking at me like I've grown a second head.

You could cut the tension with a knife. Silva probably notices it, because he says, "Um, how about you discuss this later? We should work on 'Ulterior Motive' first."

They all murmur agreement, so I agree too.

Twenty minutes later, Penny is in the recording booth playing the keyboard while Silva coaches her. Wade, Sam, and I take a break. We're by the window in an empty meeting room, and it's unusually cold here, probably because we're on the eighteenth floor. I hug myself, and Wade gives me a funny look, squinting at my jacket.

Well, not my jacket. The jacket of the girl from the club.

A grin spreads over Wade's face. "That's Cinderella's jacket!" he says.

Sam shakes his head. "I bet he'll be done with the poor girl in two dates." When I give him a blank look, he adds, "Maybe one date?"

I don't correct them. I never do. It's not worth it. Ever since the tabloids decided that me sleeping on a girl's shoulder in a club during my first month in Los Angeles was me passed out drunk with some random hookup, everyone thinks I'm a player. It doesn't help that three different girls claimed to have kissed me that night, for fifteen minutes of fame or some tabloid cash. Our band agent, Bobbi, told me to just ignore it, but it's become my whole public persona.

And I guess none of my bandmates really know me well enough to tell what's me and what isn't.

Sounding defensive, I say, "I *could* date her. Like, for real. I mean, if I knew who she was."

I don't even know if that's true. We didn't really exchange any meaningful words in my panic of running from paparazzi. But she smelled nice, and I want to, at the very least, give her jacket back.

"With your reputation, I doubt that," Sam says, while Wade scrolls on his phone. Sam is smiling his dimpled smile, and I know he doesn't mean any harm. But it's annoying.

"Found her," Wade interjects. "Well, the place where she works."

My stomach does a flip.

I was not expecting that.

"Is she one of them?" Wade asks as he turns his phone toward me.

It's a picture of five people wearing cloud-printed aprons on a diner's Instagram page. They're each holding a pin identical to the one on the jacket: a cup of coffee with a cloud drinking from it. They're all smiling, except for my girl, who looks like she might be about to commit murder. Her bangs nearly cover her eyes in the picture, but those black eyes make an impression.

My heart skips a beat. "That's her. How did you do that?"

Wade shrugs. "Just a reverse image search. It led me to the Instagram of the diner. Cinderella works the afternoon shift, according to the comments."

I look down at the jacket, biting back a smile. I almost want to hug Wade.

"Guess you have no way out now. You'll have to date her," Sam jokes.

Wade chuckles, and I frown at both of them.

"I *could,*" I insist. Even though I don't know if she would be interested.

"Sure, you could *totally* date someone for a whole summer." Wade pats my back sympathetically, locking his phone and putting it away.

Speechless, I just stare from Wade to Sam. Their lack of faith in me is astounding.

Wade has moved on already, now looking out the window pensively, but Sam's face turns mischievous. "I bet you couldn't," he says. "Do you think you could?"

Irritated, I cross my arms. "I have just said that, like, a thousand times."

Sam laughs. "So let's bet on it. For real." He pauses; Wade suddenly gains interest in the conversation again. The tips of my fingers itch, and I shove my hands into the tight front pockets of my jeans to hide my discomfort. "If you can date her all summer, we'll put 'Inconsequence' back on the album."

My throat dries. *My song?* "I mean, Silva would have to

agree to that as well, wouldn't he? He's the main producer of the album. . . ." I trail off.

"We'll fight tooth and nail for the song, as long as you win the bet." Sam smiles. "But it has to be Jacket Girl. And it's the *whole* summer, Rotten. Not one day less."

It feels like my insides are going to turn inside out. Maybe I can't do this, after all. Not because I've hooked up with so many people that it's impossible for me to settle down for that much time, but because I haven't been with anyone *ever,* and a whole summer sounds like so much time.

But.

If anything could motivate me, it's this. My song. "Inconsequence." My name in the credits.

Knowing I can't back down, I offer my hand to shake. Sam's still smiling when he grasps it, and we make the bet official. Wade even takes a picture of us to post on the band Instagram page without context, which they find hilarious.

I gulp. Ready or not, it's time to find out if Cinderella has any interest in me after midnight.

4

Sasha

The bus lets me off five blocks away from Angeles Diner, so that's how long I have to think about Lloyd's proposition from this morning. Hayley Williams screams in my ears that I'm not the big fish no more (in the real world). I don't think I've ever gotten to be the big fish, if I'm honest. I've always stayed in the top of my classes, always worked for the perfect GPA in hopes of going to college, but I've *also* always known that my chances of being able to pay for it were low.

I block out the other people on the sidewalk as I practically run past them. I'm existing in the world of the music that dictates the rhythm to which I move. That'd be the ideal, if music were the only thing that existed. No more shitty summer jobs. No more hunting celebrities in dead-end clubs to take pictures for the tabloids. That's not what Mom wants for me.

Most important, that's not what *I* want for me.

If I could be anything, if I could be the big fish . . . I would be a music journalist.

I want to get paid for what I already do for free: appreciate music. I don't want to dig for celebrity dirt. A twenty-thousand-dollar scholarship could put me on track for what I actually want.

A block away from Angeles Diner and the start of my afternoon shift, I slow down. I look up at the sky, squinting at the hot Californian sun. I've never considered myself religious, much to Mom's annoyance, but I could use a sign. It feels iffy to do this to someone, use them for a story, but if there is anyone who deserves it, it's a boy who uses everyone else.

I wait . . . and nothing happens.

It figures.

My headphones go quiet in the seconds when one song fades and the next one has yet to begin. Just as I'm about to open the door to the diner, a hooded figure bumps into me and murmurs an awkward apology.

There's a pause as he stumbles back and I take him in—a big green jacket, like he's coming from Norway or something, a black cap, and dark sunglasses.

Same sunglasses as before. And I recognize the lips.

Okay, so I know how that sounds, and that's not what I mean. I didn't stare at his lips, not then and not now. But there's a contrast between his pale skin and the pink of his lips that I can't help but notice. The shy beginning of stubble across his jawline.

I stay planted where I am and look up at the sky again. Is this supposed to be my sign?

Rotten looks at me again, this time really taking me in too, and then he smiles. "Oh, it's you!"

Because he's so full of himself, he usually never smiles to the camera. Even on red carpets and during promo shoots. Rotten always looks serious, chin slightly tilted up. It was his closed-off and arrogant demeanor on *Making Music!* that actually started his bad-boy reputation—I remember because I caught a few episodes with Mom.

So his smile now feels eerily intimate. I take a step back.

Rotten takes off his glasses, staring at me with those ridiculously long eyelashes.

Ugly he is not.

"We met at that all—"

"I remember." I cut him off. Is he stalking me? I guess this is as good a sign as any. Now I don't have to plot to find him. He's found me.

Rotten plays with the glasses in his hands as he says, "I'm sorry if this is awkward, but I came looking for you. My friend helped." He stops, looks at me. "To give you your jacket back?" I look at him; my jacket is nowhere in sight. "I mean, that's what I wanted. And to say sorry that there were pictures of us online."

Okay . . . maybe he's kind of nice after all.

I start to smile, but he quickly adds, "I wish I could *always* apologize for the trouble it causes girls when they get caught on camera with me."

So much for niceness.

He's talking slowly and deliberately, like he's being recorded, putting on a show. It's weird. Then again, he's weird.

He's also really cute, I note once again, as he bites back a smile.

"Ah, here's your jacket." He pulls his backpack to his front. I stare at his big hands as he unzips the pack and then hands me the jacket, perfectly folded. Our hands *almost* touch when I grab my until-then-forgotten piece of clothing, and he looks away.

Get a grip, Sasha. You're smarter than this.

He's trying to get to you with this fake kindness and these smiles. You've read all about it in the tabloids before. He's nothing but a player.

Lloyd's offer is still fresh in my mind. Not to mention what's at stake if I take it.

Cool. Now I'm starting to feel sick.

Rotten adds, looking earnest, "You don't have to accept my apologies, but . . . I'd love it if you said *something*." He chuckles.

Oh my God. Is he nervous? He's not nervous. He's pretending to be nervous. He's an artist. They're all actors to some extent. . . .

I frown, sizing him up. He's probably used a thousand girls already. If I use him for my personal gain too, then he had it coming.

I smile. An ear-to-ear smile.

"Apology accepted. *But* only if you buy me some ice cream."

Rotten takes his wallet from his immense jacket. I don't realize he's going through his cash until he offers me a twenty-dollar bill.

I stare at it.

"This won't do?" he asks, seeming worried. Then he fishes out his wallet again.

What in the hell . . .

I touch his arm so he'll stop, and he freezes. Maybe he wasn't expecting me to touch him? Maybe he doesn't like it when people touch him without warning first? I take my hand back and clear my throat.

"I wasn't asking you for money. That's . . ." Really weird. But I don't say that. I shake my head. "I meant we could have some ice cream *together.*"

Rotten coughs. "I— Oh, yes, okay, yes."

I pretend I didn't notice that, whatever *that* was. "I have to work now. But you could pick me up at half past six when my shift ends. We could go somewhere else for ice cream. I'm Sasha, by the way."

Rotten offers me another smile, almost shy this time.

He has a gap between his front teeth. It's really adorable.

He nods. "I'll be back, then, Sasha," he says, and puts his glasses back on.

"I'm counting on it," I say, pretending to be totally cool, and not someone who's just started their descent into being a Walmart-bin-level movie villain.

Claire is watching me like a hawk.

A little blond hawk with pink cheeks and an Angeles Diner apron, but a hawk nonetheless.

Riiiight. She must have seen me talking to Rotten.

I adjust my apron full of little clouds and angels drinking milkshakes, and wink at her. She mouths, *What was that?* but our manager, Raj, is standing too close, talking to a customer, so she can't pester me with questions yet.

I'm glad. I haven't decided what I'm going to tell Claire. My best friend has been a fan of Mischief & Mayhem since *Making Music!* Her lock screen is a picture of their lead singer, Penny, singing into a microphone with neon lights behind her. Even though Penny is Claire's low-key obsession within the group, she wouldn't be too happy to find out that I'm going to pretend-date Rotten and dig up some dirt on him. But I always tell her everything that's going on with me, and it's not like I can keep him a secret from her if we *do* go out.

Claire is practically bouncing behind the register, but I busy myself with work, aggressively cleaning up booth five. I wipe down the low-hanging cloud lamp, spray some alcohol over the wooden table, and only stop rubbing with the flannel once the table is clean enough to eat directly from it.

Usually I hate all this themed crap. The diner's sparkling-white heavenly look and bright lights mean that if anyone spills anything, it needs double the work to get cleaned.

But today has been a good day. It's a good day because

Rotten came looking for *me,* and after my shift we're going out. My one-way ticket to college has finally come, and this summer job isn't just a preview of the rest of my life. Rotten will do something outrageous and horrible enough that I can get pictures and recordings, Lloyd will be happy, and I'll be twenty thousand dollars closer to college.

Easy, right?

Finally Claire gets a break in customers and, without missing a beat, bounds over to me, where I'm still scrubbing down tables.

"Girl," she says, her voice low and serious. *"Spill."*

Claire is the sweetest person I know, but I swear, when she gets something into her head, she's like a dog that can't let go of a bone. And Rotten is one juicy, savory bone, especially for a Mischief & Mayhem aficionado like her.

Claire and I have been best friends practically forever, since some kid tried to bully her in preschool and I basically bit his head off. In fact, she's the one who got me this part-time job at the diner freshman year, and we've worked here together every summer.

It's not a matter of trusting Claire. I'd trust her with my life.

But do I want to get her involved with Lloyd's scheme?

I know the answer before the words are even out of my mouth. "There's nothing to spill," I say, shrugging. She gives me disbelieving eyes, and I continue. "I *promise.* I ran into him outside this stupid club he was at last night and lent him my jacket. He was returning it. It was nothing."

“It didn’t look like nothing,” she says, waggling her eyebrows.

I can’t help but laugh at her. “Okay, he *did* ask me out, but—”

She’s gasping dramatically before I can even finish my sentence. “He *what*?”

She practically collapses onto the table, and I roll my eyes at her, knowing I’m going to have to wipe it down all over again while I tell her everything.

Well, *almost* everything.

I reach around her and adjust the cloud lamp over the booth.

What a heavenly day.

5

Daniel

Of course I'm here thirty minutes early. It's my first date, and I was too nervous to leave the studio at a normal time. I basically spent the afternoon staring at the clock in our studio room, and when it was finally five-thirty, I was like, Why not just come a bit early? It's reasonable. Los Angeles traffic can be hell.

I parked in front of the diner at 6:03.

The windows of my car are tinted black, so I'm safe from the public eye while I needle through an attempt at a scarf. It helps with my nerves, crocheting. I guess my big sister, Helena, is going to get a new bright blue scarf, even though there's not much use for it in the Los Angeles heat.

Also helping with my pre-first-date jitters? The new music streaming from my phone.

One of the label execs does this for me—shares some of

the songs from upcoming bands they're considering signing. In return, I tell her my thoughts about them. It's refreshing to listen to people who haven't yet felt smothered by the pressure of being in the public eye. I mean, I'm new to fame, and it already feels inescapable.

I bob my head to the rhythm of a pop punk beat, heavy with drums and bass. The guitar isn't quite there yet . . . but the band has enough heart that I'm definitely going to put in a nice word for them.

It doesn't really make sense that anyone would let me just give my opinions about something like this. I definitely don't feel that I'm qualified. But as long as I'm fooling everyone into believing I deserve to be in this band and play *Rotten*, I'm going to enjoy it.

My wrist aches from how hard I'm crocheting. My fingertips—even though they're calloused from playing the guitar—still throb sometimes when I apply too much pressure to the yarn twirling on the needle. I toss the scarf onto the passenger seat and roll my wrists, swearing in Portuguese under my breath.

And then someone knocks on my window, and I jump.

Sasha.

Sasha's here.

She's staring through the window with narrowed eyes, her hair pulled back into a tiny ponytail. She knocks on the window again.

Did she see me crocheting? Oh God, oh God, oh God.

I put the scarf and ball of yarn in the glove compartment, pause the song on my phone, and unlock the door.

She pulls the passenger door open, still looking suspicious, but her eyes soften a little when she sees me. "I wasn't sure whether that was you or some creep parked here. But I figured creeps probably can't afford a sports car."

My face grows hot as she slides into the seat next to me.

"I was, um, making some calls." Making some calls? Who am I, a CEO or something? I shut my eyes for a second, regretting my word choice, but Sasha doesn't seem to have noticed anything odd. She closes her door. "Also, the car . . . It's a bit . . . Yeah. My sister wanted it, after we moved here from Brazil. We share it."

Sasha turns to me with a curious smile. "I wouldn't expect anything less from Rotten himself." I'm trying to think of something to say, but then she takes her phone out and adds, "Just going to text my mom to say that I'll be late."

Once she's done typing, she puts the phone in her lap and gives me an expectant look.

Right.

Now it's my turn.

I clear my throat. "I have an idea, if that's okay. A surprise."

She studies me. Serious for a split second, then teasing. "Woo me."

I'm not sure what that means. It's not a word that has come up in the eight months I've been in the United States, or before, studying English in school. But I nod like I understand and open Google Maps on my phone. With a proud smile, I announce, "We're still going to get ice cream but at Griffith Park."

Sasha stares at my phone for a second, then at me. "Griffith Park," she repeats slowly.

"Oh, have you never been? I thought maybe you would've, because it's such a famous spot, and you're from LA . . . I think. I don't actually know that. I shouldn't assume. Where are you from?"

Maybe I put my foot into my mouth somehow, but she still hasn't said anything else, so I don't start the car. She can leave if she wants, but I don't want her to. I want to get to know her.

And, honestly, I'd like to win the bet against Sam as well. But mostly I just want my first date to go well. I did spend a lot of time on Google, searching for "top places in Los Angeles to have a first date," and Griffith Park seemed like the perfect choice.

She looks like she's holding back a smile. "I have been there. Anyway, okay, yes. That's cool. And I am a Los Angeles resident, born and raised."

I start the car. Okay. This date is happening.

"But my family's from Brazil," she adds.

I don't take my eyes off the road except to look at Google Maps, but her comment makes me pause. I love that she's from Brazil. It feels like this may have been meant to be. Like we're connected.

"Eu não sabia que eu ia encontrar outro brasileiro aqui. Brasileira, né." I give her a quick smile.

Sasha doesn't say anything for a moment. Then she says, "Yeah, I have no idea what you just said. Was that Portuguese?"

My face heats up again. Of course she doesn't speak Portuguese. Why did I think she would? Brazilian family. Los Angeles born and raised. Start using your head, Daniel.

"Oh—" I try, but I'm not sure what I'm going to say next.

Thankfully, I'm saved.

"Um, so tell me about your family," she says.

I stop at a red light and give her a curious smile. She's holding her phone fiercely, like it might jump away from her and leave her alone with me in the car. Like it's the one thing that could save her from this awkward first-date ride.

I offer, "They're great." The red light turns green, and I start wondering what's wrong with me, that I can't keep a conversation going with someone my own age. "Thanks again for helping me avoid the paparazzi the other day, by the way. I hope that picture they took didn't cause too much of a problem for you."

She grimaces. "It's fine. You couldn't *really* see my face, so almost no one recognized me."

Almost no one. I want to ask, but she doesn't look like she wants to offer up any more information.

"Well, I have my hoodie today so no one will see me or take pictures of me. And I'm wearing all black, so I'll blend in." I turn to her briefly and catch just a hint of a smile back before my eyes are on the GPS again.

"I think you're being a little too optimistic, but I've never heard of any paparazzi going on the Griffith hike for pics, so we should be good." For a moment, she doesn't say anything else, but I'm too busy driving to look at her again, navigating the streets of Los Angeles. "We'll blend in," she adds, like an afterthought.

I wish I knew what she was thinking about. Maybe that I'm too much of a risk. Or maybe she's seen what the tabloids say about me, that I switch girlfriends every day, that I drink too much, that I party too hard.

The rest of the ride is mostly quiet.

We spend a frustrating half hour looking for a parking spot at Griffith Park until, defeatedly, I make a U-turn and leave the car curbside up a hill. The first thing I learned during that half hour was that perhaps Googling the best date spots in Los Angeles won't actually give me a secluded space, shockingly enough. Another thing I learned was that I really like Sasha's smile.

"You keep laughing at me," I say, calling her out, but I'm biting back a smile too.

She chuckles. "I mean, I was timing you in my head to see how long it'd take you to give up. We're going to have to walk, like, two miles for sure."

I take the key out of the ignition and pull my hoodie up. "Not the best spot for a date, apparently."

"Don't sound so disappointed," Sasha says. "It's going to be fun."

We get out of the car, and the cool night air takes me aback for a second.

Los Angeles evenings can often be too hot compared to my hometown, Curitiba, where it's always chilly. But tonight there's a fresh breeze that doesn't make me feel suffocated in my hoodie. I ditched the sunglasses because I knew it would get dark, but I feel a bit naked without them. Like people are going to recognize me and screw this up.

Nobody does, though, at least not at first. There are other hikers passing around us when we start up the trail, better equipped than me in my skinny jeans, but they don't pay us any attention.

I look at the girl beside me, feeling really glad that we're doing this. Going on this date together . . . getting to know each other. And I can't help but feel a little rush of adrenaline thinking about "Inconsequence" making it to the album if Sasha and I turn out to be the real deal.

She holds her phone in her hand. It still feels like she just wants to make sure there's an easy way out, but I try not to take it personally.

"Hike often?" It's not my best attempt at making conversation, but ever since coming to the US and having to practice making small talk in a foreign language, it's good enough for me.

Sasha gives me a funny look. "Yeah. Locals here are famous for being at one with nature." She pauses, then breaks into a smile. "I can't believe you're nodding—no, I was joking. I do not hike often. But I'm used to running after buses enough that I think it's going to be a breeze."

I stick my hands into the front pockets of my jeans and keep walking beside her.

"Not going to lie, I'm already feeling pretty out of shape. If I pass out, you're going to have to call the paramedics," I say.

That steals a laugh from her. I like her laugh even more than I like her smile. It's a bit loud, and she laughs with her shoulders too.

"You're an *artist*! You should have better stamina than you're giving yourself credit for."

"I don't sing." I shrug. "So I really don't have stamina."

She rolls her eyes, but she's still beaming. She bumps her shoulder against mine, and if we weren't hiking up a steep incline, I'd stop and stare into her eyes and say something really smooth. At least, that's what I imagine I would do.

"Do you— I mean— Are you comfortable with that?" she asks, after a beat. "Not singing, I mean. Are you . . . are there any conflicts in the band because of it?"

It's an odd question, but I risk telling her the truth, even though the only person with whom I've talked about this before is my sister. "There aren't any conflicts per se. But I don't really feel like I'm part of the band. . . . I don't know if you used to watch *Making Music!* but I auditioned solo. They auditioned as a band. The execs decided to put us together because Mischief and Mayhem were missing a lead guitarist, but Penny, Wade, and Sam have known each other all their lives. I'm a last-minute addition."

She frowns slightly. "What do you mean? You feel like you shouldn't be there?"

"Mm-hmm." I look at the ground, at my Converse All Stars going one in front of the other. "Ever felt that way?"

Sasha snorts, but not like she's upset at me. Like she's upset at the world.

Eventually she takes a deep breath. "So many times. Even in the smallest things . . . but you're a rock star. You shouldn't feel that way." As soon as she says it, she seems to regret it. Abruptly she says, "Hey, race you to the top. Deal?"

Very much *not* a deal—I wasn't kidding about my stamina—but I don't have the chance to say no. She takes off.

6

Sasha

I can finally put my phone away while I run. That's freeing enough, like I can stop pretending to be an undercover journalist. The wind blowing against my face as I race past casual hikers is just a much-appreciated bonus, cooling off the heat in my cheeks.

Unspoken rule number one of bringing down a player is that you can't fall for their playing. None of that getting cozy and getting to know each other. I have to record until I run out of battery on my phone. I have to take pics. I have to build a case against him. Not start talking about myself like I matter in this equation.

So I run, and it feels familiar.

I didn't lie when I said I was no hiker, but as kids, Claire and I used to run track. It didn't last long—neither of us was good enough to qualify for competitions, and soon other things became more relevant, like fantasizing about going to UCLA together.

Track felt good, though. Running felt good. And it feels good right now, even as I'm looking over my shoulder to check if there's a guitarist catching up to me. He's just a bit behind me, and I smile bitterly at that. Of course he has the stamina. Of course he lied about that too.

It's a first date with a guy who's famously not into second dates, after all.

I come to a halt when I look up at the sky.

LA pollution usually doesn't allow for magnificent views of the sky, but this is stunning. The sun is almost setting, orange and pink; it's so beautiful that I can't move for a second, just looking up at it, feeling small in the best kind of way. It's been a while since I was last at the Griffith Observatory. I forgot that there is such a spectacular view at night.

Rotten comes up behind me and places a hand on my shoulder. I flash him a quick smile before looking up again. He's breathless by my side, his cheeks turning red as he tries to steady his breath. I guess he didn't *entirely* lie about not being prepared for something like this.

"You . . . killed . . . me."

We've made it to the end of the trail, which opens up to Griffith Observatory, shining brightly at the top of the hill. There are people spread out on the grass in front of the building, some having picnics, some just chilling. With a sudden burst of courage, I take his hand in mine and announce, "Let's hide your body, then."

His hand is very hot in mine, but our fingers interlace easily.

My breath hitches. I tell myself to cut it out. It's just holding a guy's hand. Jesus, Sasha, are you seven? I've held lots of people's hands. I even had a girlfriend for a few weeks last year before she left California. Had a full-on make-out session with a theater club kid before spring break.

Holding someone's hand is nothing.

It feels like something, though.

I lead as we stroll the rest of the way to the observatory and sit in one of the ledges curving around the side of the building. It's a little obscured, a little away from the rest of people. I sit down, and I'm still holding his hand.

Rotten's breath has finally evened out after our race. The sides of our thighs touch—his ridiculously-inappropriate-for-hiking black skinny jeans against my loose denim boyfriend pants. I look at our hands together on top of my knee and begrudgingly let go.

With a little smile, I tell him, "I can't believe you took an LA local to the most touristy place in town. There's no ice cream here either, by the way."

Rotten offers me an apologetic look. Earnestly he says, "Mistakes were made."

He has an objectively perfect face, and I kind of hate it. In my defense, I can't really focus on much else, with his giant hoodie covering up the rest of him. I can only see his smile that shows no teeth, the shy stubble on his chin, his thick dark eyebrows, his almond eyes. His Adam's apple bobs when my eyes search his face, like he's nervous.

Not that he could be. But it still looks that way.

“It’s really beautiful,” I say, pointing up at the sky but still looking at him.

He looks up, frowning slightly. “Mm-hmm.”

I hum. “Aren’t you going to give me lovey eyes as you whisper, *You are?* It’s very classic-romance-movie.”

I’m joking, of course—I don’t think anyone has seriously used that line in real life. But he still seems to consider it for a moment.

“I’m much more of a rom-com guy myself.”

“Rom-coms? Really?” I raise my eyebrows.

He gestures dismissively.

But I don’t have time to press him for more info, because just then a tall man dressed in a uniform starts our way, armed with a flashlight and an expression that looks like he’s ready to kick us out of the park. Apparently we’re not supposed to be sitting here. He holds the beam directly to our faces. I pull my arm over my eyes to defend myself against the light, but I guess Rotten’s not as used to oppressive authority as I am, with his wealthy status and whatnot, because he only squints at the man.

And the man’s face turns from a scowl into a grin.

“Well, I’ll be damned. Aren’t you the snobby guy from *Making Music!*? Mischief and Mayhem?” he asks.

He says it loudly enough that a few heads turn our way.

“Yes . . . ?” Rotten tries.

Yes, Rotten. You are the snobby guy from *Making Music!* That’s you.

The guard doesn’t look like he’s going to yell at us anymore. He's smiling big. "Can I take a selfie with you? I used to play the drums when I was in high school. I even had this band and everything. We were called the Angeles of the City." He waggles his eyebrows proudly.

Rotten frowns.

Before he can say anything unkind, I add in, "That's a really good name."

Rotten gives me a look like I might be unwell.

"Thanks," the guard says, turning off the flashlight. It's the first time the light has disappeared from Rotten's face since the guard approached us, and Rotten looks relieved. "So, how about that selfie?"

"Tell you what, I'll take a picture of you two," I say, shuddering at the thought of going viral because a Griffith Observatory security guard wanted a photo op with his apparent celebrity crush and I just happened to be in the shot. It's not like he's asking *me* for a pic, anyway.

Again, Rotten gives me a look. Already there are a few phones pointed in our direction, but no one's made a real fuss about the celebrity in their midst. At least not yet. Maybe they don't know who Rotten is, just that he's sorta famous?

We both get up, and Rotten poses awkwardly next to the guard, who puts an arm around his shoulders. The guard is a little shorter than Rotten, and though Rotten doesn't flash an actual smile at the camera, he's smiling with his eyes. At me. Like he's saying, *You win this time.* I smile back as I take the pictures.

"Thanks, man." The guard nods, and when I give his

phone back, he walks away grinning, zooming in and out of his pictures. It's enough to make people start taking pictures of us.

Which reminds me: I should be recording all of this. But my phone is in my purse, not in my hand. And it may have missed everything he said since we sat down beside each other.

I go through my things until I find my phone. It doesn't matter anyway. It's out of battery.

My face falls. Now, even if I manage to coax anything out of him, I won't have proof that he said it.

Rotten comes near me, lays a tentative hand on my arm. "Hey, Sasha. You okay?"

Calm down, I tell myself. It's okay. It's going to be okay. I can figure something out.

Except I can't, because this is a guy who doesn't do second dates, and my phone's dead, and he hasn't said anything that would land me an exclusive. That would get me into college. While it may be funny that Rotten took me to one of the most touristy places in LA, it's definitely not enough for a byline and a scholarship.

My heart sinks, and suddenly I want to cry.

I really let myself think that this time things would be different. This time, I'd get what I want. I let myself dream about actually going to college, and that was my first mistake. I should know that a scholarship like this isn't just going to fall into my lap. Imagine me, going to a place like—*gasp*—UCLA. Lloyd was delusional to count on me.

It's all over. And I have nothing to show for it.

Holding back tears, I turn away from him. "Can you take me home?"

It takes him a beat to answer. Maybe he's confused, or maybe he's just pissed off.

I don't care about either possibility. If he's mad that he's wasted his time on me, I'm angry that I missed my shot at the future I wanted for myself. At least I get to end this on my own terms instead of being unceremoniously dumped by him.

"Yeah," he says slowly. "Don't worry. I'll take you home."

7

Daniel

I ruined everything.

It must've been all the people with their phones pointing at us. The bet's barely started, and I've already lost. That's what I get for being someone that phones just naturally seem to gravitate toward.

Honestly, I'm not even *that* surprised. Just disappointed.

I ask her for her address, and she puts it wordlessly into Google Maps. I follow my GPS for the longest time without saying anything, and eventually we hit traffic; everything taking a million times longer when it's the evening in Los Angeles. I'm not sure whether to be grateful for the extra time with Sasha, or annoyed because it means more awkward silence.

My hands itch for something to do. I wish I could crochet or play my guitar.

"Can I— Do you mind if I turn on the radio?" I ask.

She breathes out heavily. "I was just thinking about that. Yes, please."

Except it's not the radio that plays when I turn it on, but one of the songs recorded by a label hopeful that kicks back on when the Bluetooth connects. I don't turn it off, though, because the band is good. Good enough that they *could* be playing on the radio. Not that I think the label wants to take risks with this type of different, innovative sound.

"This is really good," Sasha says, after the first minute. "I can't believe I'm saying this, but *who are they?*"

We stop behind a Mercedes-Benz at a red light, and I turn to her with a smile. "Why can't you believe you're saying this?"

"Because I know about music," she answers. "You know what, I'm not going to reframe that. I really do know about music. It's not like we're going to see each other again, so I don't have to worry—"

"We're not?" I interrupt her.

I mean, I figured that I'd done something wrong when she asked to be taken home and was silent the whole ride back. But hearing her say this still stops me in my tracks. I didn't . . . She seems like someone fun, and I thought she was having fun with me too.

And then there's the bet.

Sasha gives me a brief look, then turns away to the window. We're still stopped in traffic, so it's not like the sedan next to us has much entertainment to offer.

"Yeah, like, I've heard that you don't bother with second dates." She shrugs.

I want to ask her where she's heard these things, but the answer is obvious.

My old friends: the tabloids.

"I mean . . . I *was* hoping for a threesome with that security guard at the observatory. That's just how I roll," I comment, gesturing dismissively. She turns to me with wide eyes. Still earnest, I add, "I am joking."

She chuckles, still looking uncertain.

The light turns green, and my attention shifts forward.

As the band continues singing from the car speakers, I say, "They sent their demo to my label. One of the execs showed me. I like their sound a lot, but even though I've listened to this song so many times already . . . I can't figure out what's missing. The exec told me their chances aren't very high because the sound isn't mainstream." As another joke to help lighten the mood, I add, "Perhaps a music connoisseur like yourself can help me give them a fair shot."

Sasha is quiet for a minute.

Her silence grows for so long that I think she hasn't heard me. Or maybe she's fallen asleep. (Am I really that boring?) But when I look at her, she's deep in thought, staring at the console of the car.

Then, suddenly, she says, "It needs neon."

"It needs neon," I repeat. I'm sure she can hear the question in my voice. Maybe this is an American thing.

"A neon vibe," she explains, like this makes perfect sense.

"A mix of rock and disco. A synthesizer could make the song poppy enough to play on every radio station and still maintain the original sound."

"Hmm," I say. Maybe she's right. I'm still not sure about the whole *neon* thing, but a synthesizer could take the song to the next level. It's definitely worth bringing up to the label. I give her a sideways look, and she smirks back at me. "How do you . . . ?"

I'm glad she seems to get what I mean even as I trail off, because I'm not sure how to express it. *How do you talk about music as if it's a visual thing?*

"I'm going to be a music journalist." Then she seems to hear herself, makes a face, and explains, "Eventually."

"I'd like to read your pieces."

"Maybe," she says, sounding like she absolutely means no. "I'd really like to cover Brazilian artists. Like I told you, I'm Brazilian."

I nod. "Where are you from?"

I catch a shift in her expression. "I'm from California."

"Okay." I frown. "But in Brazil, where are you from? I'm from Curitiba, Paraná."

Sasha grunts. "I can't believe you're one of those people who are really weird about diaspora folks."

I glance at her. "Um. I . . . I'm not sure what *diaspora* means. Like, the word."

She pauses. "For real?"

I don't know why she thinks I'd joke about this, but Sasha seems to really think that's the case, because when I give her a serious "For real," her voice changes again. Not as hard and defensive.

"It's when people aren't from their original country. Like, their families immigrated." Sasha pauses, and a little more assertively, she adds, "And sometimes people like you, who were born in Brazil, make it seem like people like me, who were not, don't have the right to Latinidade."

"No, no, I didn't mean it like that, I promise." I turn to her, and she points at the road. *Eyes straight ahead, buddy.* "I wanted to know where your family is from to see if maybe I've been there or . . . I don't know. Curiosity."

I can't tell if she believes me. She's probably had so many shitty encounters with other people from our same community that her assumption was the default.

Sasha is quiet for another moment. "I don't know. Mom's grandparents immigrated. It was a long time ago, and I guess that information got lost. I don't like to think about it." She adds, "I don't think I ever met another person of color who didn't know what diaspora was."

"Oh, I'm not," I reply immediately.

I hadn't thought that would give her pause, but apparently it's a sensitive topic. When I glance at her, she's got an eyebrow cocked. "What is that, Latino boy?"

I take a deep breath. "I mean," I start, "I guess I understand that I'm read as a person of color here. But I lived most of my life in Brazil, where I had plenty of white privilege." I let go of the steering wheel with one hand, gesturing to myself. She can't have missed my pale skin tone. "So it's . . . strange. It feels like I'm not being truthful if I say I'm a person of color, because I had white privilege growing up. It feels dishonest." I frown. "But also, now I'm in this industry . . ."

She finishes my sentence for me. "That will never see you as white."

"Yeah." I shrug.

"There is still privilege for being a light-skinned person, obviously. I know what you mean," Sasha says. "You don't have white features, and you have a thick accent, but if you keep your mouth closed, maybe you could pass for white. . . . But I'm a brown Latina. I'm a person of color wherever I go."

"Right. So I feel like it's weird, having all this privilege, and saying I'm a person of color."

We're quiet again for another beat.

"Look, you can say you're a white Latino if you want, but with your accent, I don't think any American will ever see you as anything but a person of color." She touches my arm. "That's not a bad thing either. It's just a thing."

My arm is in flames. My face is hot too.

But right now, looking at me this way, she seems to want me to know I'm not alone. To just be there for me.

I clear my throat. "Is my accent bad?"

She removes her hand from my arm. "It's actually really cute."

"But do I pronounce things wrong?" I murmur. "Is my intonation off?"

Sasha grunts. I sneak a peek at the GPS. One minute until we reach her house and say goodbye.

I want to make the most of this. Of every moment with her.

"No. Well, maybe sometimes you do. I don't know. I don't care." She shrugs. "So what if you get some words wrong sometimes? So do I and everyone else who was born and raised here too. It's part of how language *works.*"

Suddenly my throat is dry and my eyes sting.

I have flashbacks of all the English classes where I did less than amazing. All the hours studying vocabulary on apps on my phone, multiple textbooks, memorizing song after song so I'd get the perfect intonations.

Will I ever get to a point where I'm flawless? Reach fluency? Be mistaken for someone whose first language is English, instead of someone who copied irregular verbs as a kid to memorize them?

"Don't stop talking because you have an accent, okay?" Sasha asks.

"You reached your destination," the GPS robotic voice says.

I slow the car to a stop.

I've been quiet in my public life because I didn't want to get things wrong. Because I'd rather not put myself out there. Can she tell? Does she know me that well already?

Sasha touches my shoulder, tentatively. "Your accent is part of who you are."

She sounds so kind and loving that part of me wants to

bring her face closer to mine and kiss her right here and right now, in the dark of my car, outside her house.

"And that's not a bad thing either?" I ask quietly.

As if reading my mind, her hand slides up from my shoulder to my neck, the warmth from her touch raising goose bumps on my skin. She cups the side of my face, and I lean into it, staring at her.

"It's just a thing," she answers, slightly above a whisper.

"Okay." I breathe in. "Just a thing."

Impatiently Google Maps repeats, *"You have reached your destination."*

But my mind's spiraling—I want to get to know her better, and I want to talk about music with her. I want to ask her what she thinks of Mischief & Mayhem, but also, is that too self-centered? I want to ask her for music opinions and compare them with mine. I want to ask her if she knows any of the Brazilian rock I grew up listening to. Did she think Cazuza *made* rock 'n' roll or is she more of a Renato Russo kind of person? Did she ever listen to Garotos Podres and TNT? Was Cássia Eller on her radar at all?

"Cometomyparty."

Sasha raises her eyebrows. "What?"

I clear my throat. "Come to my party," I repeat. "I'm having a party at my house. A pool party."

I'm not, actually. I just need a reason to see her again, and this was the first thing that popped into my head.

Way to go, Daniel.

I set my jaw. I try to keep breathing. My fingers are gripping the steering wheel so hard that my knuckles are paper white. I look back at Sasha, trying my best not to look like a weirdo. "You can bring a friend."

"A friend," she repeats.

I'm inventing a whole party so we can see each other again, and that's the part she focuses on? All right.

"A friend." I nod, suddenly realizing that *I* don't actually have friends to invite.

This may be a horrible idea.

No, it's definitely a bad idea.

"When?" she asks, after a beat.

"Uh, Saturday?" I offer tentatively.

Her face falls and her shoulders sag. Wait, did she really want to say yes? "Oh, Saturday." She takes a deep breath. "I'm sorry, I—I can't. . . . I'm working a double shift this Saturday."

"Saturday. Did I say *Saturday*?" I force a nasal laugh. "That's so funny. I meant Sunday. I love Sundays."

I love Sundays?

"Okay," Sasha says, a smile spreading across her face. "I'll go to your party. Guess I should get your number then, huh?" She tilts her head, hair swaying. It's such a specific type of smile that it takes everything in me not to grin like a fool.

"Yeah. Let's—let's do that."

8

Sasha

I'm writing numbers on the spreadsheet on my clipboard, clicking the pen in my hand a few too many times while I'm checking the ice cream stock in the walk-in freezer at the diner, because I'm so distracted. I have to count again several times to make sure I didn't mess it up.

I thought I'd royally screwed up by not having my phone charged for my date with Rotten, was sure I'd have to kiss college goodbye . . . and now he's invited me to a *pool party.* I'll make sure to bring an old-school recorder this time. No way I'm making the same mistake again.

Lloyd called this morning, asked me about the date at Griffith Observatory and said he'd seen some pictures of the date circulating but they were too dark for him to be sure it was me. He was thrilled when I confirmed it was, like I was about to deliver the story of the year. I told him about the pool party, and he gave me instructions to take pictures of Rotten's house. I don't know what he expects me to find—some *Fifty Shades of Grey* room attached to the kitchen? But I'll follow through, of course.

I'm fantasizing about college classes and future music journalism internships when I realize that someone's watching me. I nearly jump when I see Claire hanging out by the entrance of the freezer, shifting her weight to the other foot.

"You still haven't told me about your date with Rotten," she accuses, half joking, half tiny ball of excitement.

"There's not much to tell," I answer, my back still turned to her. "I told you everything in my text. He took me to Griffith, we hiked, we sat around for a little bit, and then he took me home. End of story."

My robotic version of events doesn't seem to faze her. Claire comes closer and bumps her shoulder against mine. When I hold back a smile and don't respond, she does it again, more exaggeratedly this time, and whines, "Sasha! Come on! He came to pick you up at work! I want details. Are you and Rotten dating?"

I don't know what to say. "No, we're not dating"? "I'm just trying to get enough dirt on him to write an exposé for LA Now"? Or "Yes, we are dating, since I'm invited to this party he's throwing, and he told me to invite a friend, but I don't know if I should involve you in this mess"?

"I would've never guessed that my best friend would be dating *the* Rotten!" She dances around me, grabbing my inventory clipboard. When I motion to take it back from her, she winks at me. "I got this. Think of it as a treat for nabbing the hottest rock star I've ever seen in my life."

I laugh. "You make it sound like dating Rotten is a privilege, like he hasn't dated half of Los Angeles." I raise my eyebrows, trying to make light of it, even if it bothers me more than I'd like to admit. But I guess it's okay that he's using me. After all, I'm using him too.

Claire nods, but then says, "It's just, he's never been photographed with anyone on an actual *date* before. You must be special to him."

I've seen the pictures of our Griffith Observatory date on Twitter. Mystery girlfriend strikes again, people are saying. I'm grateful for the unforgivingly dim lights of Griffith at night. You can't tell it's me at all. But Claire knows, of course. She's the one who sent me most of the low-quality pics of us sitting together outside the observatory.

"I'm not *special to him,*" I say, mimicking her dreamy tone. "Actually, I still can't believe we're having a second date."

She gasps and drops the clipboard on top of an ice cream box to come and hug me. I'm still processing that I said that out loud when she squeezes my shoulders. "Sasha, dating *you* is a privilege. And you two are totally dating, by the way!"

I feel a little sick. Maybe it's from being inside the freezer for so long.

No matter how much I love Claire, I can't forget that she's practically a superfan. She's got Mischief & Mayhem posters on her bedroom walls and YouTube playlists full of compilations of the band from when they were on *Making Music!*

I shouldn't do this. I shouldn't involve her.

But. She would have so much fun.

She's still hugging me when I blurt out, "Do you want to go with me to this pool party at his house tomorrow?"

Claire's jaw drops.

"Oh my God," she says. Then again, a little louder, "Ohmy*God*. Are you serious?" I start to reply, but she interrupts me. "*Would I like to go?* Of course I'd like to go! I'd love to go! Sasha, that's so cool!"

Claire smiles from ear to ear and bounces on her feet. Then she hugs me again.

Oh, yeah. Involving Claire is definitely *not* going to blow up in my face.

9

Daniel

As we're hanging out by the pool on Sunday morning, my sister, Helena, doesn't react the way I thought she would when I tell her about the impromptu party we're throwing. Instead of looking confused, she giggles and studies my face, like she's searching for something I'm not saying. My face burns and I look away. "What?" I murmur.

"I'll help you. I'll even invite Otis and my friends. But I want to know why." After a beat, she adds, "It's not like you to throw parties, period. But especially not like *this*."

I could argue with her. After all, a pool party in the height of the summer is perfectly reasonable. And our band has been feeling the pressure to finish the album soon, but with four more songs to record, we're running on coffee and anxiety, and we need a break to just relax. Which is true. But unlike my bandmates, Helena *knows*-knows me. She'd see through me in a second.

So I don't lie. "I met a girl. Her name's Sasha."

"Sasha," she says, drawing out her name like she's testing the word on her tongue. "Do tell."

Because I'm not sure what to say without bringing up the bet, I dodge her questioning look. "I do need you to invite some friends, by the way. I'll ask our agent, Bobbi, to see if she can invite some clients in town too. I don't want to look like a loser with no friends."

"Um, way to change the topic. Really sells the fact that you're not hiding anything." She swings her legs in the pool, apparently finding this hilarious. "And you're not a loser. You're just selective about your friends."

"Helena, I have no friends," I deadpan.

She rolls her eyes. "You're throwing a party. You're going to make more friends." Pausing, she gives me a look. "I talked to Mom on the phone earlier today. She says Los Angeles is changing you."

Helena's got one eyebrow raised and she's half smiling. She looks just like Mom, minus the wrinkles and pitch-black eyes. Helena's are the same hue of brown as mine, and her hair is a dyed dark red, while Mom's is almost black.

"Me mudando?" I frown.

"Speak in English," she reminds me. "You'll never feel comfortable talking in English if you keep talking in Portuguese whenever you have the chance." Then she nods. "But yeah. In a good way. You should tell Mom that you're throwing a party."

I stare at the water below and tentatively swing my feet

into the pool too. It's cold, but on such a hot morning, it feels good.

I don't want to talk to Mom about this. It's already embarrassing to ask for Helena's and Bobbi's help inviting people, because after eight months, I only know the people in my band. I haven't made any real friends in the US. And that's not something I want to bring up to my mom. I want to show her that I'm doing well. That uprooting Helena's life was worth it.

When I passed the online audition for *Making Music!*, Helena put college on hold, packed her bags, and offered to be my guardian. Since she's five years older than me, she has always sort of acted like I'm hers. It wasn't that big a surprise when our parents gave me their approval, as long as she was going with me.

It *was* a surprise how fast she learned English. How fast she made new friends at her new college, how fast she found a boyfriend—Otis, a very tall fat guy with tattoos on his arms and an easy smile, who doesn't seem to care in the slightest that I'm in a reality-show-famous band—and made herself a new life.

Meanwhile, I still feel like I'm swimming against the current, struggling to fit in.

"I'll buy flamingos," she decides.

I frown at her, but she misses it, looking up at the sky with a big, grateful smile, bathing in the Los Angeles sunshine like she was born for this. And maybe she was, much more than the chilly breeze of Curitiba, where we had to hide under heavy jackets and umbrellas all the time.

It's funny to me that she thinks I've got myself figured out, that I'm *living my truth,* just because I know I'm demisexual. I've known for a while now, and I don't feel like that made me some self-aware love guru. Between the two of us, she's still the only one who knows what she's doing.

"And we need rules," she continues. "No one enters the house. It's all outside."

"Are you finding your calling as a party planner?" I ask.

She ignores me. "Otis can come in the house, of course. And your girl, if she wants to."

"She's not my girl," I correct her. Again, she doesn't pay me any attention.

"But other than that, nobody else comes inside. We don't want to risk anyone drenching our red carpet." It's not a red carpet, it's a dark red rug, but she likes to pretend it's fancier than that. I smile at her, because it's difficult not to, and nod. She leans closer and says, "This will be epic, Daniel."

I'm glad that the first person to arrive is Otis, wearing a floral shirt and carrying four inflatable flamingos. Helena wraps her arms around him, and after some PDA, they're ready to finish setting up our impromptu party. Helena has already decorated the backyard in dim yellow Christmas lights, with a giant pink flamingo neon silhouette in front of a Brazilian flag just beside our back door. Otis also brought the umbrellas for the lemonades.

Helena made a whole lot of lemonade, Swiss and plain, and I'm on my third glass when Penny arrives. She's wearing a pink swimsuit and has her matching pink locs wrapped in a bun on top of her head. When she sees that we're the only ones here, she immediately apologizes for coming too early.

She takes her phone out, and suddenly Wade and Sam are here too.

After that, it's half an hour of people I don't know arriving and me trying to act cool and composed while I down three more lemonade cups, almost choking on a little pink umbrella. Five of Helena and Otis's friends arrive, then three more, but Sasha still hasn't come.

Helena prepared the playlist; a summery electronic beat is playing, and I'm trying my best to drown my nerves in the music, watching these people I don't know play around in my swimming pool. This is Helena's party, not mine.

The only people I know—my bandmates—are nowhere to be seen. Last time I spotted them, they were squished together on the patio furniture, watching TikToks on Penny's phone. In other words, they're doing their own trio things, and once again, I'm feeling left out . . . at my own party.

"Boo!" Wade yells behind me, and I jump, nearly dropping my lemonade. I give him a death glare.

Wade smiles easily, flashing dimples, and runs a hand over his messy dyed white hair. "I'm sorry. You just looked so focused. Are you waiting for your girlfriend?"

"Girlfriend," Sam contributes with a snicker, coming up behind Wade. "How's the bet going, by the way?"

I give him a tight, toothless smile, and turn back to Wade. "Not girlfriend *yet.* But she's coming soon. I think." *I hope.* She hasn't texted me since she told me she was coming, over an hour ago. Not that I've been checking my phone.

Wade looks smitten at the very idea of this, but Sam rolls his eyes with an all-knowing smile. "I'm going to go get drinks," he says. "Your sister's cool, by the way."

"My sister has a boyfriend, by the way," I add.

Sam raises his eyebrows and drifts away from our group, lifting a hand in a farewell salute. I really hope he doesn't take my words as a challenge. He's too young for Helena, and Helena's in love with Otis, but there's nothing I'd hate more than a bandmate dating my sister. The thought makes me nauseous.

I stare down at my lemonade. I hope Sasha arrives soon.

"Um, where's Penny?" I ask Wade after Sam departs, just to have something to ask.

"Networking, probably." Wade shrugs, and without warning, takes off his shirt. He's not as muscular as Sam, who is leaner, but he still looks good enough without a shirt on that I feel myself grow smaller in mine. "I think I saw her with Nati earlier. Wanna hit the pool?"

I backtrack.

"The pop singer Nati?" I frown. Bobbi told me that she'd extend the invitation to some of her other clients, but I didn't really think I'd know anyone. Nati is Brazilian too. Way bigger than me, an actual international sensation, but still Brazilian. "She's here?"

Wade nods. "Yeah, she came with her boyfriend and a few friends, but I don't know where they are now." He searches the crowd for a second, stretching his arms as he gazes around, seemingly uninterested in the fact that someone way more famous than us is in our vicinity. He adds, "Hey, next week we're going to this skateboard park near my house. . . . You should come."

I cringe. They do this every once in a while—offer half-hearted invitations to hang out separate from band stuff. It's not that I don't appreciate the gesture, but it always feels like they're just waiting for me to say no. And I'm not looking for pity invites.

"Ah, I'm sorry. I . . ." I trail off, watching his expression change from uncertain and hopeful to disappointed. Is he actually disappointed?

It's not that I don't *want* to hang out with them. Saying no is my knee-jerk reaction. But maybe I should stop saying no to them. Maybe . . . I should give this a shot. Give *them* a shot.

I clear my throat. "I would love to go, actually."

Wade's bright dimpled smile comes back. "Cool, cool." After a beat, he adds, "Hey, don't tell Sam I said this, but I'm totally rooting for you to win the bet."

He gives me a sheepish smile.

I clutch the plastic cup in my hand a little tighter, not knowing what to say.

"Sam's my best friend, but he's a cynic. I'm a romantic!" Wade declares. "Now let's get to the pool already! I want to cannonball into this Olympic-sized monstrosity."

"It's not Olym—"

He ignores me, sprints away, and jumps into the pool, drenching everyone who was standing close by.

A blond girl, one of my sister's friends, is one of those unlucky bystanders. She looks like she's ready to bite someone's head off, until Wade gets out of the pool, throwing his head back, his white hair just long enough to be combed back as he gives this girl his winning smile.

The girl melts, waving hello at him.

He winks.

A romantic, all right. I laugh.

10

Sasha

Claire and I stand side by side in front of an enormous two-story house, awestruck and unmoving. It's boiling outside, and these sandals hurt my ankles, but I wanted to look *pretty*. I am wearing pink, heart-shaped sunglasses—Claire forced them onto my face. And though I didn't bring my camera, I have my phone in hand and an old-school recorder in my purse, and I'm ready to go undercover.

I was going to wear my school swimsuit from two years ago, but then Claire called twenty minutes before we were scheduled to take a car to Rotten's gated residential address. She gave me a disgusted look on video and coerced me into putting on a black-and-white polka dot two-piece. This is more me anyway. But I feel weirdly vulnerable, even with the loose white dress on top.

I state matter-of-factly, "We should ring the doorbell."

She takes a deep breath. "I'm taking a mental photograph. I'm outside Rotten's house. From Mischief and

Mayhem." Her nostrils flare, and her whole face turns pink. "Do you think there will be drugs here? My mom's going to kill me if she smells marijuana on me."

I chuckle. "Girl, what are you talking about? You live in Los Angeles."

Claire still looks concerned, but she doesn't have much time to mull this over.

Because, just then, Rotten opens the tall oak door. My heart leaps to my throat in a hiccup. An *actual* hiccup. I cover my mouth.

Shooting me a warning look, Claire murmurs, "Stop."

Hic.

"Oh my God, Sasha, that is *Rotten.*"

Hic.

She slaps the small of my back, *hard.* No more *hics.*

"Hey, I'm glad you could make it," he says.

I don't see who he's looking at, or where his eyes go, because he's wearing those dark shades from the first time we met. I suddenly feel ridiculous about these pink heart-shaped sunglasses.

It's already dark, just past sunset. None of us should be wearing sunglasses.

His biceps flex when he moves to scratch the back of his neck. That move is definitely on purpose, and I'm not fool enough to fall for it. I don't care for the toned arms, don't feel even a hint of curiosity at what his chest looks like under that inconvenience of a shirt, and I'm not ogling his thighs peeking out from his swim trunks.

"This is my friend Claire," I say, with a nonchalant smile plastered on my face. "Claire, this is . . . Well, you know who this is."

Claire absolutely loses her cool and *giggles.* It's disconcerting. She then proceeds to wave at him, and he reluctantly waves back, like he's not sure exactly what the right move is.

I don't blame him.

"Nice to meet you, Claire." Little smile. Corner-of-the-mouth type, not a full-on smile showing his teeth with the little gap. "So!" He brings his hands together, rubs them. They're nice hands. Musician hands. "Let's go to the back. The backyard. The pool?" He motions with his thumb and offers another corner-of-mouth smile.

Then he leads the way.

Claire grabs my arm. "He's so cool," she whispers.

"Kind of a weirdo," I reply to her, and she lets go of my arm.

I've seen the insides of rich people's houses before, and I've seen their pool parties. It may not have been *in person,* but I have. A few weeks back, Cindy at LA Now wrote an article about a coke party at a B-list star's house, and I got to see literally hundreds of pictures before she and Lloyd settled on the ones they'd publish on the website. I have my phone in hand, and I won't disappoint them. I'll take as many pictures as I can.

But this doesn't look anything like the celeb parties I've seen before.

There are pink flamingos. Everywhere.

It's not just the four—*four*—floating inflatable flamingos in the swimming pool. There are tall drinks with flamingo umbrellas, toy flamingos that are half my size staked around the backyard, and pink flamingo towels draped over beach chairs.

"I love flamingos," Claire murmurs.

I don't have the time to respond to that, because Rotten's looking back at us, spreading his arms and saying, "Welcome."

There's around twenty people mingling in the large backyard, and I recognize a few of them immediately. A tall tanned girl who has the same gap between her front teeth as Rotten, but none of his mysterious demeanor, is sitting under an enormous parasol—not flamingo-themed. It's the Brazilian flag. She's wearing a bikini with a ring of pearls around her waistline, and she has a single dot of gold as her belly button ring. She's talking to someone who looks her age, a fat man with luscious hair, brown skin, and thick sunglasses. They're both staring at us without making any effort at pretending like they aren't.

I've seen her in Rotten's Instagram stories. She's his sister, Helena. And the guy is probably her non-famous boyfriend, who I've also seen in Rotten's stories.

Sitting in a nearby beach chair is internationally acclaimed DJ Lotus, wearing a neon-green bikini, her unevenly cut short black hair shining under the patio lights. A girl with light brown skin and fake-blond hair is sitting on her lap, wearing a matching neon-blue bikini. They're oblivious to us, as is English indie film star William Ainsley, who's having a drink and a chat with Mischief & Mayhem's Sam, both looking completely immersed in conversation.

In the water, Mischief & Mayhem's Wade is floating near a blond girl on one of the flamingos, his pale arms resting on her tanned legs as he looks up at her, openly flirting. I don't know her from any magazines or influencer accounts.

Finally I see possibly the two biggest stars of the place, sitting side by side right in front of another Brazilian flag: Penny, the band's lead singer, and Brazilian American pop star Nati, leaning on the other like they're best friends.

I am entirely out of my depth.

Even though there are strangers here too, this is a backyard of famous people. The combined net worth in this place is probably the equivalent of a small European country or something.

I shoot a nervous look over to Claire, hoping some of that telepathic connection we used to have when we were kids is still here, but she's giving Rotten heart-eyes. She probably hasn't even looked around yet.

Rotten pushes his sunglasses to the top of his head and gives me a smoldering look that makes me forget we're in this yard full of famous rich people.

"Can I get you something to drink, Sasha?"

I wonder how many times he's asked girls this, looking at them like they hung the moon and the stars. I cross my arms, squinting at him. "Sure. I'll have whatever you're having."

He nods, gesturing at one of the lawn chairs and telling

me to make myself comfortable. As I sit and he goes to get my drink, I see his sister walk over to him and stage-whisper, *"Which one is she?"*

Oh my God. What has he said about me? Have they made fun of me together?

Claire plops down into the seat next to me and squeezes my arm. "I can't believe this. He's so cool and you're so cool and he's getting you *something to drink,*" she trills in my ear. I swat her hand away, but there's a smile playing on my lips when I see how excited she is. "I can't believe you're going to put Los Angeles's biggest player on a leash."

Chuckling, I shakc my head. Taking advantage of this moment away from Rotten, I open my purse, set the recorder to start, and take my phone out. Claire doesn't see any of this. She's completely starstruck.

When we were little, we used to dream of going to UCLA together. Claire had an aunt who went there when we were young and took us on an extra-official campus tour. We were in love with everything, even the dorms. We fell for the buildings and the benches, sitting on the grass under a tree and staring up at the Californian sun and feeling at home.

We fell in love with the idea of being close to our families too. Claire wanted to live in a dorm but come back to her parents' house every weekend. I wanted to still live with Mom, because even then I knew that'd be the most realistic option. We both worked hard to get good GPAs and do application-worthy extracurriculars. I have the school newspaper and debate, and Claire has chess and soccer.

Before Lloyd and his scholarship came along, I eventually realized that college was going to be financially unattainable for me. But it was never unattainable for Claire. It was always a sure thing. That's probably why we don't talk about college as much as we used to when we were younger. She must know my chances of getting a scholarship are low.

Rotten comes back with two plastic cups of lemonade, one for each of us, but his eyes are trained on me. It's kind of cute. I like the way his hair looks with the sunglasses holding it back.

I bite back a smile, realizing only now that I've been staring at him the same way that he's been staring at me.

Claire clears her throat. "Um, I'm going to show myself around."

Taking a sip of my drink, I put my phone away. With the recorder on in my purse, I lean closer to him. "So what's in this?" I eye my drink curiously. What are the chances that Rotten has a fully stocked bar in his house? Probably pretty good, I think. Maybe I could get pictures later.

Rotten pauses. "It's . . . lemonade."

"Yeah, but." I shrug. "With?"

"Lemon and water. And sugar. And ice."

I narrow my eyes, trying to scan him for humor, but he just flashes me a smile instead. If this is sarcasm, it's a weird way of showing it. But there's his nice smile again, with the gap between his front teeth and all. I glance down at his mouth.

He clears his throat, looking away.

"Can you introduce me to your friends?" I ask, as innocently as possible.

And he nods, because why wouldn't he? It's not like I'm out for blood and headlines.

The party is in full swing when Sam pushes for Rotten to bring his acoustic guitar down. Helena gets excited, and they bring down three. One for Rotten, one for Penny, and one for Nati, because as an international pop star, of course she'd get a guitar as well.

I'm curious. I didn't even know Nati could play. Huddled on a pile of beanbag chairs next to the pool, they murmur to each other before Penny sings the intro to a Dua Lipa song, and Nati follows along. Rotten comes next, missing a few notes but laughing when he does. I'm more into it whenever he gets something wrong, because his endearingly embarrassed expression is worth it. It's so obvious that it's because he's not super familiar with the song of choice, and not because he's not good enough at the guitar. He's actually totally at ease with the guitar on his lap, calloused fingers running up and down the body of the instrument.

But Penny and Nati never miss a note. Their fingers move fast, like the guitars are extensions of their bodies, and their voices fill each other's out like they've been singing together forever. I could see a future collab working out.

My pop music knowledge is limited, but I know enough to know that almost everyone loves Nati. And because she's the only Brazilian in pop with major name recognition, everyone just assumes she's the embodiment of what Brazilians are.

I resent that. Mom and I don't look like her, and neither of us had her upbringing. I resent the Portuguese words she inserts into her songs, and how everyone swoons now when her voice starts filling the void left by the other guitars. I don't even like it when Penny joins her, and their voices mix together so well, Rotten's fingers moving through chords, an expression of pure joy on his face.

It's not that I'm jealous. Or, well, I'm not jealous because of him, not really. He looks so in his element that it's beautiful. But I'm jealous of this other girl, who gets to claim whatever she wants, while I'm sitting here, holding a cup of lemonade, feeling like an outsider.

"I'll be right back," I whisper to Claire.

I don't know if she even hears me. She's transfixed by the next song, one of Nati's singles that she released last year. Claire is singing along to random Brazilian words that I can't even pronounce.

Nobody pays me any attention as I wander off. I can't be there anymore; it feels suffocating, even though we're all outside and the breeze is light and cool.

I take my phone out, pretending to text, and snap some

pictures of the scene—the three stars strumming their guitars, their famous friends clapping and singing along, having the time of their lives. My mind's not even fully in it yet.

I'm feeling a weird sense of not-here-ness.

If I go to college, will I feel like those people by the pool? Will it be some magic fix? Will I feel that sense of belonging?

I see more partygoers coming in through the gates, and with no one to welcome them, they just come closer to enjoy the impromptu acoustic set, attracted like magnets. How many people has this guy invited?

I stare up at the house and feel a pull to look inside. An invitation that's not from Rotten or Helena, but from Lloyd. I hear his voice in my head, telling me to take initiative, to make things happen.

Looking over my shoulder to make sure nobody is noticing me, I slip inside.

I'm not sure what I'm looking for yet, but I'll know when I find it. In the meantime, I take pictures of everything, until it looks like I could sell this house just from my photo gallery.

The kitchen is relatively small and extra organized. The living room looks cozy, and that takes me aback. It's not the magazine-ready room I thought it'd be, impersonal and plastic. There are woolen blankets on the couch, one a deep blue, the other gray. The lights are dim and warm, and although the TV is ginormous, there are cups of tea scattered on the little glass-top coffee table, and rings of coffee mugs marking it. Hardly scandalous enough to make front pages, but it makes me smile. Mom would kill me if I left rings like these on furniture.

"I was wondering where you'd wandered off to."

"Jesus!" I scream, turning around and accidentally pressing the camera button.

The unexpected flash makes Rotten blink a few times. He sits on the couch, looking stunned.

"Oh, I'm sorry," I try, sitting beside him on the couch. "Are you okay? That was—that was a complete accident. I wasn't trying to take your picture, I swear." Which is technically true, but I'm not sure how to explain that I had my camera open in the first place.

Rotten is still blinking at nothing when he chuckles. "It's okay. I shouldn't have startled you." It's funny how he says *startled*. It makes him sound so much older than seventeen. "Were you looking for the bathroom?"

"Yes," I say, too fast. I take a deep breath and will my heartbeat to slow, then look at him. He brought one of the guitars back; it's sitting by his side on the couch. I stare at it for a second, then say, "Got tired of playing?"

"Oh." He picks up the guitar and brushes his hand over the smooth wood, like he's caressing a pet. "Yeah, they're still going outside, but I wanted to put my favorite guitar away. I don't even know why I brought it out in the first place. Got carried away, I think."

"Your fans seemed to love it," I tease.

He shrugs.

I put my phone down a little awkwardly, remembering the recorder still going in my purse, and point at the rings of coffee on the table in front of us. "Your parents don't mind?"

Rotten hugs his acoustic guitar. "They would, if they were here. I think."

The truth is that I already know he and Helena live alone. It's not super difficult to find this type of information online, and even if it weren't, Claire volunteered every Rotten fact she knows on the ride here.

"I live with my mom," I blurt out, hoping he'll feel comfortable enough to open up to me. And because he gives me a look like he *does* feel comfortable, I somehow find myself saying, "Dad bailed a long time ago. He's not in our lives."

Rotten looks at me. "His loss. Clearly."

That makes me smile. It also makes me roll my eyes. "Cheesy!" I retort. He chuckles at me. "So you don't live with your parents. Are they in Brazil?"

"Yeah. Helena and I would never be a good enough reason for them to give up their own lives."

I find it so funny how he uses perfect grammar sometimes, like saying *Helena and I* instead of *Helena and me,* like most people I know. I'm a little caught up in that, and in the way he strings his fingers along his guitar without much care, so I only register how big this revelation is a second later.

"Why do you say that?"

"We weren't ever a huge priority for them." Rotten presses his lips together, and then adds, like an afterthought, "It's not like we were ever neglected or anything. They're very much in love. There just wasn't a lot of love left for us. But I've always been close with Helena, so." After a beat, he adds, "Mom and I used to be closer. Nothing happened, but it's like we couldn't connect at all anymore as I got older. She taught me how to make these." He points at the blue blanket that covers the back of the couch.

His words hit me harder than I expected they could. I can't imagine Mom losing interest in me. We're so close. It makes me sad for him that he feels that way, whether what he says is true or not. Part of me knows I should press for details because this conversation is being recorded, but another part of me just feels for him.

Instead I point at the blanket and ask incredulously, "You *made* these?"

He nods, staring straight ahead, cheeks pink. "I crochet when I'm nervous. Or bored."

A rock star who crochets. It's kind of cute, but also so at odds with his public bad-boy persona.

"You're staring," he says. I start to apologize, and he shakes his head. "No, it's okay. Just don't tell anyone, please. People will think I'm strange."

He's still not looking at me, so I bump my knee against his. "It may ruin your player image. Give you a bit of a heart."

Rotten finally looks at me, giving me dead-serious eyes. "And we wouldn't want that, would we? Not if I'm going to seduce everyone within a forty-mile radius."

His sarcasm makes me laugh. I wish it didn't come so easily. I shake my head to clear my thoughts and change the subject.

"Can you make me a pro guitarist in one night?"

Rotten offers me a winning smile. "I can make you a pro at Nirvana's 'Come as You Are' intro."

"Good enough," I say. "Come on, let's see it. Teach me your ways."

First Rotten gives me the guitar. I've never held one in my hands. It feels too big and foreign. He tells me about the arm of the guitar, what each break stands for, and where I should hold the strings. When I keep staring at him, he touches my hands and places my fingers where they're supposed to be.

His touch is calm and warm, his eyes patient and trained on the guitar, on the way my fingers sloppily grasp at the strings.

It's only two chords, but with his face so close and his calloused hands on mine, it's a Herculean effort for me to stay focused.

In the short time we've known each other, I've never seen him so collected. His mastery of the guitar, along with his patience for teaching me some of the basics, makes him fifty times more attractive to me than he already was. His hair, which has never looked bad, now looks irresistible, and all I want is to lose my hands in it. When he licks his lips in concentration, it's taunting.

I take a very deep breath, and my hands still against the guitar strings.

"I think you're ready to join the band," he teases, offering me a good-natured smile.

We haven't stopped gazing at each other, and he's just a breath away. Carefully I set his guitar on the floor in front of us, feeling my heart race.

Rotten's still watching me with those big brown eyes, blinking slowly.

I can't help it—I'm drawn irresistibly closer to him.

I am going to kiss him.

11

Daniel

I don't know what's going on.

Sasha looks at me, tentative and determined all at once, but her resolve seems to gain strength with every passing millisecond—and I swear, I can feel *every* millisecond, like we're in slow motion. My heart skips a beat, and my eyes trace her bare brown shoulders, then move up to her face, her short hair . . . and that expression.

Does she want to kiss me?

"If you're going to keep playing, I wouldn't recommend you buy a guitar like this." I point nervously at the guitar on the floor in front of us and clear my throat. This is okay. I got this. *This is okay.* "Um, it's a good guitar, I love this guitar. But it's a bit . . . pro. Not that you couldn't turn pro if you wanted."

I don't think she's listening to me, but I'm not sure, because my eyes are still on the guitar. My mind is completely consumed by her. Her, Sasha. Not *her* the guitar. The guitar isn't a her. Even though in Portuguese nouns are gendered and *guitar* is a feminine noun. So it could be a her. In Portuguese.

Oh God. I need to turn off my brain.

Maybe I could tell her that—about the guitar and Portuguese versus English. Cool. That's a good plan.

When I raise my eyes to look at her again, Sasha is close. *Too close.*

She leans in, lips ready to touch mine.

"Ahh!" I yelp, ducking so abruptly that she nearly bumps her chin on my forehead. I force myself back on the couch, putting space between us.

Her eyes are the size of tennis balls.

"I'm sorry," she nearly screams, jumping up. Her face turns red. "Excuse me, I— Gotta—"

She tries running, but the guitar is in the way.

Sasha trips on my favorite guitar, and lands spectacularly on the floor.

"Oh my God, Sasha, are you okay?" I ask, leaping up from the couch.

Sasha raises her head, looking at me like a deer caught in the headlights. "Fine." She rushes to sit up, but winces in pain, touching her ankle. "I—crap, my foot."

She looks like she's both horrified and pissed. I'm not sure if it's at herself or me.

I look around for someone to help. But everyone's outside, having fun.

"We need to take you to a hospital." I kneel next to her. "Okay?"

She blinks, looking away from me. "Okay," she grunts.

Okay. I can do this. I take a deep breath. "Can you walk?" She tests her ankle, putting weight on it, then winces and shakes her head. "Okay, no worries. I'm going to scoop you up, all right?"

I wait for her to nod again. She looks even more annoyed now, but murmurs, "Yeah."

Then I wrap one arm around her back and the other below her legs, and pull her up. She's lighter than she looks or I've got some adrenaline going—either from being almost kissed and then *yelping* or from the whole injury thing. I grab the car keys and my wallet on the way out of the kitchen.

Once we're outside, everyone looks at us. There's even more people at the party now than there were when I went inside to put the guitar away, but I barely register the sea of unknown faces. All I see is her friend Claire running up to us, asking, "What happened?" I don't even catch what Sasha says in reply.

All I know is that soon enough, I'm setting her down on the passenger seat of my car, and all three of us are headed to the hospital.

Not how I expected this party to go. At all.

12

Sasha

Watching Claire's starstruck-ness melt away on the ride to the hospital while she grills Rotten for details about what happened is the only thing that keeps me sane. All he can manage to tell her is that we were in the living room and then I twisted my ankle. Fair enough.

It hurts, but the pain dulls the longer we're in traffic, and by the time we reach the hospital and I'm taken to the X-ray room while Claire gives my info at the desk, I'm more overwhelmed by embarrassment than anything else.

Later I'm sitting on the hospital bed while Rotten paces around the small area enclosed by the curtains. There's a nurse with us, hiding her smile behind a clipboard, glancing at Rotten every other minute, but he seems oblivious to her obvious attention. It's annoying, but Claire is giving the nurse enough of a death glare that I don't have to.

Rotten's nervous pacing is making *me* nervous.

"It's just a sprained ankle," I tell him. "It doesn't even really hurt anymore."

"Shouldn't we call your mom?" he asks.

"No," Claire and I say at the same time.

Rotten shoots us a confused look, and Claire comes closer to my bed, murmuring, "But your mom's going to notice it sooner or later."

I shake my head. "Aspirin will do the job. She doesn't have to know." Rotten's look turns horrified when I say this, so I explain, "I just don't want her to worry—she's got enough on her plate as it is. Anyway, you saw the result of the X-ray yourself. It's just a little—"

"Sprained ankle," the nurse offers. I had already forgotten about her.

She's swooning at Rotten, even though she's definitely in her late twenties and he's seventeen. Gross. I roll my eyes, exchanging a look with Claire that absolutely communicates what I'm thinking. She narrows her eyes at the nurse in a superb *Can I speak to your manager* impression, and asks, "Can you give us a moment, please?"

The nurse doesn't look super happy to leave us alone, but she does.

My ankle doesn't look that bad. Swollen, but nothing's broken and it'll be as good as new in a couple of days. I wonder if Rotten's feeling guilty, even though I was the one who tripped on his guitar. His expensive guitar. After he dodged my kiss and yelped.

God, I hate tonight.

Rotten meets my eyes, and I look away, feeling my face burn.

"Um, I'm going to . . . I'll just go and pay the hospital bill, okay? I'll be right back," he says.

Claire and I nod in unison, and the second he leaves and the curtain closes again, she turns to me with wide eyes. "What the hell happened? I was living my dream watching a jam session of M and M and Nati, and then suddenly Rotten comes out with you in his arms!"

She's speaking so fast that it takes me a second to catch up.

"I tripped and fell." It's the truth, but it feels like I'm lying, so I add, "That was *after* I tried to kiss him and he basically shoved me away."

Claire slaps my arm. *"He shoved you—?"*

I groan. Before she has the chance to launch an online campaign to cancel Rotten, I clarify, "He didn't actually shove me. But he didn't want me to kiss him. I tried to leave. This happened." I point at my swollen ankle.

Claire frowns. "That doesn't make any sense. He's clearly into you."

I shrug. "Is he? I don't know. I thought we were having a moment, but now I don't know anymore. He didn't even want to kiss me."

Saying it out loud is liberating somehow. I wonder if the recorder on my purse still has any battery, and if it's capturing my words. Is this the big break I was waiting for? Teen journalist gets rejected by rock star?

"But he *likes* you," Claire insists. I groan again. "No,

don't make that face, like you don't care. It's okay to care. And it's okay to be confused."

"Maybe he just wants to be friends," I offer, but then I remember the way he was looking at me when he was showing me the chords. How his eyes looked lost in me, like he was seeing something out of this world. It's not the way friends look at each other.

When Rotten comes back, I ask, "Can you take us home? Claire's sleeping over at my house, so it's only one stop."

Claire exchanges a look with Rotten. I don't know what they're telling each other, and I'm too tired to try to find out.

"It's not so late, though," Claire tries. "Maybe I could take a Lyft home if you two want to hang out?"

Rotten opens his mouth, but I cut him off.

"I just want to sleep," I say. What I mean is *I just want to go home.* But it's almost the same thing.

"Okay," Rotten says. "I can take you home."

I try not to think about how disappointed he sounds.

I nearly jump in surprise when Claire enters my room with a singsong "Wakey-wakey, sunshine" and a package of crackers in one hand.

"Oh my *God,*" I bark, then pull the comforter all the way up to cover my head. She pulls it back down, and I'm confronted by her big smile and the light streaming in from the window. "You're so creepy. Who's this cheerful early in the morning?"

She offers me the crackers, and I take one. "It's past noon," she observes.

"Your point?" I ask with a mouthful of crackers.

She rolls her eyes at me. "Your mom already left and asked me to tell you she's doing a double shift today." She pulls her feet up and sits cross-legged on the bed. "I haven't told her about your ankle, but you should."

Oh. Yeah. *That.* Claire and I didn't talk much last night because I was so tired, mostly emotionally.

But now it's a new day, and she looks chatty.

"I feel fine," I say, which isn't entirely a lie. My ankle doesn't hurt as much, and it's looking less purple than yesterday.

She cocks an eyebrow. "Okay," she says, then hands me another cracker. "Have you told your mom that you're dating a rock star? Because I haven't either, but you probably should also tell her that."

I take my time chewing that cracker.

"We're not dating," I say eventually. "He didn't even want to kiss me. And you know, considering his reputation . . . that's pretty much a slap in the face." Pausing, I frown at her. "What's wrong with me that he didn't even want to *kiss* me? Do I look disgusting or something? He's hooked up with half of Los Angeles!"

I'm frustrated and annoyed and . . . Claire smiles. What's

she smiling for? "I don't know why he didn't want to kiss you, but I promise there's nothing wrong with you. Maybe this is about him, not you."

"Whatever." I grab the cracker package from her and shove two into my mouth.

"Whatever? So you don't care?" she asks.

"Not in the slightest," I reply.

Claire nods, sighing. "Then I guess it's no use telling you that he texted me this morning."

I sit up straighter, my eyebrows shooting high. "He *texted you*? My corpse hasn't even cooled, and he's already trying to get with my *best friend*?"

Laughing, Claire slaps my arm. "He texted me because he wanted to know if you were okay." She eyes me, then continues. "I replied that yes, you were, but why didn't he ask *you* instead, and he told me that he'd texted but you weren't responding. Asked if you were upset with him."

My eyes widen, and I reach for my phone, but it's not on the floor next to my bed like it usually is.

"It's charging in the kitchen," Claire tells me.

"Well, what did you tell him?"

She smirks. "I said I didn't know, but I asked him if you had any reason to be upset with him. . . . He said he didn't know either."

"He doesn't know," I repeat incredulously. "I can't believe he texted me anyway. We don't text. I mean, he sent me the address to his house for the party, but that's it." Claire puts another cracker into her mouth. "Would you like me to go get your phone?"

I stare.

She smiles again. "On it."

ROTTEN:

Hey! Everything okay?

Just wondering how you're doing.

ROTTEN:

This is Rotten, by the way. Not sure if you had my contact saved.

How's your ankle?

ROTTEN:

Good morning! If you haven't blocked my number or anything, I'd love to go out with you today.

Like, if you have time and your ankle's not hurting too bad.

Is this weird? Sorry.

I have the day off btw.

Claire practically melts as she reads the texts over my shoulder. "How adorable," she sighs.

It's not *adorable,* per se. . . . It's sweet. There's a difference, I think. Puppies are adorable. Being adorable is effortless. You just are. But sweetness takes effort.

I hate that I'm smiling at his messages.

I don't know why he wants to go out again when last night he wouldn't kiss me, but maybe there's still something there. Maybe I haven't completely blown my shot at this scholarship yet again. Maybe today I'll get to be the cutthroat journalist I was born to be.

I quiet the butterflies in my stomach and take a deep breath, resting my phone on my lap.

"Claire, I'm going to need your help. I need to look *irresistible* today."

13

Daniel

Sasha is stunning.

She's always pretty, but there's something different today. I'm not sure what it is exactly. Her hair looks a little wavier, her eyes a little darker. When she waves hello as she waits for me to open the door of the car, her lips look like they're made of dark red velvet. She's wearing high-waisted denim shorts with black boots, and a black crop top that reads *DON'T ASK ME WHERE I'M FROM.*

She catches me staring and raises an eyebrow. "Rotten, my face is up here."

I blush furiously.

"I wasn't . . . ," I say, unsure of how to complete that sentence. "Um, hi. I'm glad you could come."

Sasha sits next to me in the car and takes a deep breath.

"Is your ankle okay?" I ask. She didn't mention it in our texts. All she said was that I could come pick her up at seven p.m.

"Took a painkiller. Almost as good as new." She winks at me.

"That's good." I don't remember her winking before. I don't remember this whole wave of confidence that seems to make her three times hotter than she was already. I'm not sure what's going on, but I kind of like it. "I was looking online at some places we could go, and—"

"I was thinking we could go somewhere Tripadvisor may not know about," Sasha says. I chuckle and open the GPS in the car console, giving her an expectant look. She shakes her head. "I'll be your copilot. I'll give you directions, and you follow."

"Okaaaaaay."

She directs me onto the freeway, and then we're cruising. We're silent for the first five minutes except for her giving me directions. It's a little weird. I've got about a thousand disaster scenarios piling up in my head. That maybe she hates me now because of what happened yesterday at the party. Maybe Claire hates me too.

I also can't stop thinking about the bet, which Sam won't stop bringing up. In the group chat this morning, Sam kept saying how much he "bet" that Sasha and I had probably had a romantic time at the hospital. Penny doesn't actually know about the bet, as far as I can tell, which just means that Sam is being a jerk, as usual.

Thinking about it now doesn't help my nerves, though, so I turn on the radio.

And that's when things start to get normal again between us. When the radio host calls out a new block of 1990s ballads coming up, we exchange a look of mock interest. And then, when LeAnn Rimes's "How Do I Live" starts playing, we offer commentary like we're music critics.

"The melody doesn't fit the voice, so I'm not sure," I say.

"It's a missed opportunity with the high notes. It doesn't fulfill the song's true potential," Sasha jokes. "It's a no from me, LeAnn."

I nod. "We're left wondering, *What is really behind this?*"

And then Backstreet Boys' "As Long As You Love Me" comes on. She turns to me, like she's waiting for my diss, but I just turn the volume all the way up.

"What?" I shrug. "I'm no hater. This is a classic."

We stop at a red light.

"Although loneliness has always been a friend of mine . . . ," I start singing, and she laughs, nodding along, dancing in her seat.

I know I'm no fantastic singer, not nearly as good as Penny or Wade, but I'm having fun, and I hope that's enough. I plead, "C'mon, sing with me!"

She shakes her head, still giggling. "No way. No one wants to hear my singing voice. It's a torture that I'm not going to put you through."

I don't pressure her to sing, so she just watches me belt out the song instead, as she grins.

The way that smile dances on her face only makes me want to sing more.

She tells me to park on what looks like an ordinary street near the coast. You can see the ocean in the distance, but we're too high up for a good view. We get out of the car, and I look around. A few shops, some people walking by. Still nothing that makes this place look even remotely remarkable.

Sasha watches me with a little knowing smirk. "This way." She points at the gates that separate the sidewalk from the sea.

Frowning, I follow her, until we're close enough that I can finally understand.

Below us are giant pieces of concrete, broken graffitied walls, and fragments of old pavement that jut up at odd angles, making impromptu skateboard ramps and seats closer to the ocean, where groups of friends and couples are clustered. Trees and grass grow up in the cracks, like nature has completely taken over. It feels like everyone is in their own private world.

I suck in a breath. "Where are we?"

She grins and ignores my question. "Give me a hand?"

Sasha gestures at a fence that's wrapped around the park area, blocking our entrance. I give her a boost, then watch as she climbs the barrier.

"Isn't this trespassing?" I ask.

On the other side of the fence, she turns to look at me

over her shoulder. "I wouldn't have thought that trespassing was too hard-core for someone whose nickname is *Rotten*."

My face burns, and I jump over the fence too. These jeans are a bit tight for jumping; once again, I clearly haven't dressed well for our date. "I did *not* choose to be called *Rotten*," I say as I come up next to her. "It's really dorky."

She searches me with her eyes. "What do you want to be called?"

Her question throws me off.

I thought she'd ask me what my name is. This feels more personal.

"Daniel," I reply.

"Well, Daniel," she says, "allow me to introduce you to my favorite place in Los Angeles, home of creatives who don't know what they're doing, and everyone who'd rather watch the ocean than watch their ceiling at home. Daniel, this is Sunken City. Sunken City, this is Daniel."

She spreads her arms wide, and I bite back a smile.

I guess *this* is what happiness feels like.

14

Sasha

I lead him past fallen structures of asphalt and forgotten concrete, and we make our way carefully through the rocks until we're facing a wall entirely covered in graffiti. There are some people around, but they don't seem to care about us, and we don't care about them.

Rotten—no, Daniel—helps me sit, and we stare out at the ocean for a minute.

Eventually he asks, "How did you know about this place?"

This isn't the time to think about how genuine he sounds, how I want to scoot closer to him for warmth as the cool breeze comes in from the sea. No, I'm on a mission. This is my chance to get the info I need for my article, and this time I'm not going to mess it up.

"Claire's dad has a photography blog. He used to take us here a lot when we were younger." Daniel nods, like he wants to ask more, but I don't give him the chance. Instead

I ask, "Where did you use to go when you were younger? Did your sister or your parents take you anywhere special?"

He considers this for a moment, looking at his white leather Converse. "I didn't go out a lot, I guess. It's not that there weren't things to do in Curitiba, but my parents were always busy and Helena had an actual social life."

"Oh, and you didn't have one?" I tease.

Daniel offers me a half smile. "Something like that."

I place my purse between us, the recorder on, and my mind races a million miles per hour. I barely even notice the ocean in front of us until Daniel murmurs something I don't understand in Portuguese under his breath, staring in awe.

It *is* beautiful, and it smells like salt and home. For a moment, I lose myself in the moment. Everything is weightless. My college scholarship slips from my mind and I don't even care.

For a split second, that is.

"This place is my secret." He nods, like he understands. "That means you owe me a secret too." Though I try to make it sound playful, I'm aware of how demanding and borderline desperate I sound. To smooth things over, I clear my throat and add, "Um, so you have to tell me something embarrassing."

Daniel's expression lightens at this, and he chuckles, looking up at the sky.

"Oh, I'll give you embarrassing . . . ," he says. "I learned to play the guitar to impress a girl, and she rejected me big-time, in front of everyone." He sits up straighter. "This was in my old high school, back in Curitiba, right. I've always been really into big romantic gestures—"

I interrupt him. "You're not serious."

"I'm dead serious."

Suspiciously I say, "Go on."

He smiles. "I've always loved romantic comedies. Especially the ones from the '90s and early 2000s. Mom had a VHS collection, and when Helena was younger, she went through a phase of digitizing everything."

I study him. "Couldn't you find the movies you wanted on Netflix or something?"

"But you're missing the romanticism of it!" he says. He's full-on smiling now, and the gap between his front teeth makes him all the more charming. "She'd burn those DVDs and let me work on the art for the covers. Some of them were really impressive, I'll have you know. . . . My favorite movie was *10 Things I Hate About You*. Absolute fave. Have you seen it?"

I think about young Daniel lying on a carpet, playing with colored pencils. Biting back a smile, I shake my head. "Not really. I know what it's about, though. When we studied *The Taming of the Shrew* in class, our teacher said it was a popular adaptation." I stop talking and realize that Rotten's staring at me. I shrug. "What can I say? I'm not a superfan of Shakespeare *or* cliché late '90s aesthetics. Sorry, Daniel."

He scoffs, "You don't have to like any of these things. *10 Things* transcends them."

I have to suppress a laugh. He looks extremely serious.

"As surprising and interesting as it is to find out that you're a '90s buff, you were talking about that time you were dumped?"

"I'm not a '90s buff," he protests. "I like romantic comedies specifically."

"Back to the story!" I demand playfully.

Daniel takes a deep breath. "Okay, so in the movie there's this *epic* scene. . . . Heath Ledger steals the microphone and sings to Julia Stiles at the top of his lungs in the middle of their futebol practice. It's, like, the sweetest moment of the whole film."

Oh my God.

I get a sense of where he's going with this.

"No, Daniel. Please tell me you didn't try to reenact something like this."

He smiles. "The song is 'Can't Take My Eyes Off of You.' "

Shaking my head more vehemently now, I murmur, "No."

Daniel nods. "I spent *weeks* learning how to play it on the guitar and memorizing the lyrics in English. Then I walked into her volleyball practice with the guitar in my hands. . . ."

Covering my mouth to muffle the chuckling, I say, "I want to disappear on her behalf. I'm afraid to ask, but I need to know. What happened?"

"At first she tried to pretend like I wasn't singing to her. And, because I apparently couldn't take a hint, I kept playing and actually said her name. Eventually she turned red and walked away."

Daniel shrugs as if saying, *It is what it is.*

Between my fingers, I say, "This is mortifying!"

"It really was," he agrees. He groans good-naturedly and smacks himself lightly on the forehead.

"Incredible." I make a face at him. "So you got into music to get girls."

"To find love," he corrects me.

It's the right thing to say. It makes my cheeks burn, even though I know about his reputation. Looking away at the ocean again, I say, "You're such a player."

You can't hate someone for being who they are. But you can kick yourself mentally for falling for it for the third time in the past half hour.

"That's not true."

He sounds frustrated, and also . . . close. Dangerously close. But I've already been rejected by him once, so I keep my eyes on the ocean straight ahead and ask, "Why do you like romantic comedies so much?"

Daniel thinks for a moment.

"They're fun. There's always more than meets the eye, but you can expect a happy ending no matter what the characters are going through."

"Not like real life," I add.

He raises an eyebrow. "Why can't that be real life?"

I snort. "Well . . . Maybe it can for people like you, but not for people like me."

I know why I'm sitting here, sharing a sacred place with him.

I mean, look at me right now. I'm here on assignment to find dirt on the dirtiest teen rock star. I'm not going to be just another girl who falls for Rotten's nice-guy routine. I'm going to go to college, and it'll be UCLA. I'm going to get this scholarship and fulfill a dream I didn't think possible.

Most of all, I'm not going to make Mom's mistake and fall in love. I've seen what happens when you love someone who doesn't seem capable of loving back.

For a split second, it's like he can read my mind. "I'm sorry your dad left. Not everyone is a jerk," Daniel says.

He reaches for my hand, tentatively at first. Then, when I don't yank it away immediately, his fingers intertwine with mine.

I look at our laced hands and swallow away the bitter taste in my mouth. "When you say it like that, it seems like you're a non-jerk who wouldn't leave someone you care about."

The corner of Daniel's mouth goes up just a bit. "I'd love to be a not-leaving non-jerk."

A little red in the cheeks, he beams at me.

I know it's an act.

But watching him gaze at me so earnestly, while Sunken City changes from sunset to evening, the stars peeking out in the sky above us, it sort of makes my heart ache anyway.

15

Daniel

"How are things with your girl?" Helena asks, instead of asking how I slept, or why I woke up at one-thirty after staying out late with Sasha at Sunken City last night.

Groaning in response, I sit beside her at the kitchen table and reach for some carreteiro. It smells and looks amazing. The scent is rich with leaves and pepper, and the rice is a faded hue of red, mixed with spices and fried ground beef. She puts a hand up when I try to reach out for the pan, though.

"Manners, Dani. Your big sister asked you a question."

She seems to be having too much of a good time with this, and I'm too hungry to play games, so I relent.

"She took me somewhere cool yesterday. We talked for hours. I took her home. There you go. Can I eat now?"

Helena puts her hand down so I can get myself some carreteiro and takes a sip of her orange juice. "Love how you keep me in the loop. So many details, I don't even know where to focus." I smile at her, and she adds, "I just want to know that you're happy with your girl."

"Sasha. Her name's Sasha," I tell her.

But I consider her words.

The thing is, I've known that I was somewhere on the asexual spectrum ever since I was young. I do get attracted to people, but it isn't immediate, and it definitely isn't based on looks alone. I knew Sasha was attractive the first time I saw her—I mean, my eyesight works just fine. But it's different, recognizing someone as attractive in general, and *feeling* attracted. I need a little bit more *something*—time, intimacy, whatever. But whatever it is, I feel like it's happening now, for real.

"Saaaa-sha," Helena singsongs, like she's an annoying younger sister instead of my twenty-two-year-old guardian. I avoid her eyes and focus on my food, and I hear her chuckling. "I'll stop now, don't worry. Um, we have a video call with Mom and Dad later tonight."

I'm glad she stopped talking about Sasha, because the more we talk about her, the more I feel like I should tell Helena about the bet. Even though the bet is such a small thing. I'm not *forcing myself* to be with Sasha because of the bet. The bet was just an excuse to talk to her in the first place. To have my first girlfriend.

But I wish Helena had gone in a different direction with the conversation.

"Can't. I have a thing. It's a band thing," I clarify.

Helena sighs. "Daniel."

"It's true!"

"I didn't say it was a lie." She makes a face. "It's just . . . I know you don't love the video chats. I don't either. But they're our parents."

"And it's the mandatory weekly chat so they can check that item off their to-do list," I offer.

She doesn't smile, but she doesn't tell me I'm wrong either.

After another sigh, she says, "I hope whatever you're doing today is important."

I nod. "It is."

I wasn't lying to Helena. Even though maybe for her it wouldn't be that big a deal to just hang out with her friends, for me this is major. It's the first time I'm hanging out with the rest of the band outside of rehearsals, and I'm hyper-aware of how new and weird this is.

When I get to the skate park, all three of them are already on their skateboards. We're the only ones in the place, which is nice—I don't need any cameras on me while I embarrass myself skating.

Penny's hair is up in a knot, and she's wearing a neon-orange crop top with black leggings. Wade is in all black, with a long T-shirt that makes him look shorter than he really is, and his white hair is standing out. Sam is wearing a loose sleeveless shirt with a skull on the front, and denim skinny jeans.

After quick hellos, Wade announces, "Just so you know, what you've got is not a skateboard. You bought a longboard."

I look at the board in my hands. Now that I'm scoping out mine next to theirs, I can see that theirs are slimmer. "That's not so bad, right? The one I bought looks easier to ride than yours."

"Yeah, you made a good purchase," Penny says, and smiles.

"Accidentally," Sam adds.

"I hate riding longboards." Wade shakes his head. "The wheels are too soft and big. It's bouncy, horrible for basically anything that isn't going in a straight line." I stare at him, and he flashes me a smile. "But I guess going in a straight line is more important for you now than doing an ollie."

Not sure what an ollie is, I nod along. Then I set the longboard on the cement ground and take a deep breath. "It doesn't seem so hard." I step on the board with one foot, and it rushes ahead, nearly making me lose my balance.

Sam hides a chuckle. Wade grins. I side-eye them both.

"I can do this," I announce. This time I try to catch the board and step on it. One foot, then the second foot, and miraculously I'm standing on the board. I feel like I'm Tony Hawk. "Told you I could do this."

"Nice!" Penny claps. "Now try to move."

Sam drops his skateboard to the ground, pushes off, and sails by me. I try to mimic him, and this time I actually *do* lose my balance. I don't fall to the ground, but it's still frustrating. I curse, shaking my head, and Wade pats my back.

"Hey, hey. That was good! You're doing it!"

"Obviously not," I protest. "I don't think I can do this."

Sam looks over at us and says, "Guide you in your journey, we will."

Wade agrees. "Best mentor ever. I'm Obi-Wan Kenobi, obviously."

I blink slowly. Is this a reference to an anime they've watched together?

Penny rolls her eyes, but she's beaming. "Dorks."

They flash devilish grins to each other. I'm too confused to ask, and they're too busy getting excited about how they're going to teach me how to become one of the greats.

Wade tries to teach me how to do an ollie, and I fail categorically.

But it's kind of fun, I realize, while falling for the second time.

He offers me his hand up, and we try again.

Again and again and again, until we're sitting side by side on the grass, Penny absent because she went to get more water, but the three of us are drinking energy drinks. Watching the sunset, too. It's nice.

"How's your love life?" Wade asks, raising his eyebrows.

The way he asks it makes me laugh. "Summer isn't over yet, but we're still a thing." It's not entirely true, but it's not entirely a lie either. I'm not sure Sasha would say we're a *thing,* but would she say we're not?

On Wade's other side, Sam nods. "I saw the speculation online, people saying she broke her ankle last week at your party. Did she?"

"No, just sprained it, but she's fine. We've been texting every day." Then, after a beat, I ask, "What are people saying?"

"People say all sorts of things." Wade shrugs, then gets up. "Don't pay attention to people."

Penny rejoins us with her bottle of water full again. "Why shouldn't we pay attention to people? What's this about?"

Sam, Wade, and I exchange looks. I'm not sure how she'd feel about the bet we made for a song to be on the album, but I don't think she'd be too pleased.

Wade clears his throat. "Nothing specific, just in general," he says. "Any of you want to join me for another ride before the sun sets for good?"

We shake our heads.

As Wade takes off, Penny sits on Sam's other side and takes a sip of her water. "Tomorrow we'll have a long day at the studio. How are you feeling about the album?"

"I'm too tired to feel any kind of way," Sam says, and groans. "It's been day in, day out. I swear Silva wants to keep us there until midnight every day."

I smile to Penny. "I'm actually pretty excited. Can't wait to hit the studio again tomorrow."

Sam makes a sound of annoyance, and Penny glares at him.

We're silent watching Wade do tricks and fall off his skateboard. Sam is better than him, much more skilled and focused, but watching Wade is more fun. He makes up for his lack of technical expertise by making silly faces and swearing loudly every time he gets something wrong. Penny takes pictures of Wade, and Sam uses his arm to shade his face against the sun, yawning.

I take this time to do a little Google check to see what I supposedly shouldn't pay attention to, what people are saying about me and Sasha. When I search my name, I see photos from the night of the pool party. In the pics, you can tell I'm carrying a girl to my car, but Sasha's face is buried in my chest; you can see her short brown hair but not her face. One outlet says that my new girlfriend jumped from the balcony into the pool and broke her ankle. It says it was the wildest party of the year.

Yeah, not exactly. Still, I'm glad her face isn't visible in the pictures.

I lock my phone again, just as Penny's vibrates in her hand. "Oh, it's Mom. I gotta take this. Be right back." She slides her thumb on the screen and walks away, chatting animatedly into her phone.

We watch her go a little farther from us, and I ask Sam, "I know you've been friends since high school, but how long have you all known each other exactly?"

Sam's eyes are still closed against the sun when he replies,

"Wade and I, middle school. We met Penny in freshman year of high school."

I take a deep breath. "Was it hard? Getting on to the reality show?"

Sam pulls himself up to sit cross-legged. In a robotic voice, like he's answered this question a million times before, he says, "It was a priceless opportunity." When he meets my eyes, he cracks a smile. "It was bullshit for a long time, trying to make it onto the show with just the three of us. I thought the producers weren't going to do anything with our band. Then you came, and they decided they wanted us after all."

I can relate—it wasn't great for me either. I auditioned countless times for different execs and then celebrity judges who didn't even necessarily know anything about my music genre.

I was good enough that they flew me from Brazil to the US after watching my first tapes, but not good enough that I could go anywhere on my own. I only became worth noticing when they put me with Mischief & Mayhem.

And then we became a thing. Reality-show stardom, or whatever.

All any of us wants is to be taken seriously outside of that. To be a seriously good rock band, regardless of where we came from.

We're quiet for a moment, and Wade is still too entertained with his skateboard to notice any tension between us on the sidelines. I keep thinking of how much fun I was having until Sam and I were alone.

After a long pause, Sam says, "I should've brought a soccer ball since you were coming."

I open and close my mouth. I didn't expect that kind of comment.

When I first moved to the US, I barely went online, and my agent, Bobbi, seldom let me know when someone said something microaggressive about me. I wasn't really aware of being Brazilian before coming to the States. I grew up where everyone was Brazilian. I wasn't *the* Brazilian one.

But here it's different. I just can't believe I'm getting it from my own bandmate.

I sigh. "Yeah. Because Brazilians love futebol."

Sam raises one eyebrow, then looks away from me. "You don't, apparently."

"I don't want to argue," I say.

He looks genuinely surprised. "I was just kidding."

I turn to him. "So should I always bring you a burger because you're American?"

Sam just presses his lips in a thin line, then rolls his eyes.

"I feel like," I start, taking a deep breath for courage, "you believe some stereotypes about Brazilians, and stereotypes can be really . . . patronizing . . . and . . ."

"I know what stereotypes are, thank you very much," Sam replies, his tone dry. "I said I was just kidding. I wasn't trying to fight." He takes a very deep breath. "Wade said I should try to connect with you. This was me trying."

Looking back at Wade, I notice he does seem to be glancing our way often.

Did he and Penny plan this? To give us alone time to talk through things?

Even more horrifying, was this really Sam attempting to be nice?

Then Sam throws himself back onto the grass so he's staring up at the sky. "I'm sort of Brazilian too. But not really. . . . Like, only sort of."

I blink a few times, surprised by this turn in the conversation. But I'm listening.

He continues, "My grandfather immigrated during the dictatorship, but Mom was always all-American. Never had a Brazilian name, and apparently her father wasn't all that great anyway. He died before I was born." Sam sighs. Then he sits up again and looks at me. "Mom doesn't call herself Brazilian, and Dad's a blue-eyed white guy. So I'm not exactly Brazilian, or Brazilian American, or whatever."

I take a deep breath, nod in acknowledgment, and then look out at the expanse of the skate park. I search my brain for the best words.

I don't know the best words. In English or Portuguese.

"I'm not going to tell you who you are, but if you ever feel like reconnecting with your Brazilian heritage, you have the right to that too." I pause, looking at him. "And I'd love to help if I can, with anything."

Sam regards me for a second, his expression more serious than I've ever seen it.

Then he breaks into a smirk and says, "You're offering to be my Brazilian Yoda? Rotten-Yoda. Ryoda, if you will."

I blink. "You mean . . . the baby?"

Sam frowns. "Oh my God, Rotten. Is your only Star Wars knowledge *The Mandalorian*? Have you never . . ." He trails off, shaking his head in disgust, but his tone is different. It's teasing, fun, almost like how he talks to Penny and Wade. He makes a funnel with his hands and yells, "Wade! Get over here! We need to educate Rotten on movie classics!"

"*Educate* me." I snort, rolling my eyes. "I'll tell you what's a classic . . ." But I don't, because he's too excited, and Wade's skating back to us and calling Penny over.

We don't talk about what it means to be Brazilian or not anymore, and it doesn't seem to occur to Sam that me not being super well-versed in *Star Wars* is because I grew up with entirely different pop culture references. But we stay in the skate park until the mosquitoes start to get ruthless. I miss an inside joke here and there, but overall, it's not so bad.

It's not bad at all.

16

Sasha

It's usually not very quiet in the house when Mom and I are home together, so I'm enjoying this moment of peace. The two of us are squeezed on the love seat in the living room, making judgmental comments about the rich characters in the soap opera we're watching. They always make the most obviously wrong choices. We love to think we'd do differently.

She's been working more than usual this summer, taking on double shifts at the superstore. I think it's because she feels the pressure of my senior year coming up. This is the last summer when she can dream that she can save enough to send me to college.

It's not fair to her, or to me.

But when we're like this, my feet thrown onto her lap, and her tossing her hair as she mimics a character in the soap, I'm not thinking about money.

Until my phone rings.

Mom reaches for my phone on the floor and makes a face when she sees the screen. "It's Lloyd. That's your boss at LA Now, right?" My eyes widen, and I sit up straighter immediately. "Maybe he's got some new job for you. You haven't taken pics for them in a while."

She offers me a hopeful smile as she says this, which of course breaks my heart.

I hate keeping things from her—her *and* Claire. And yet.

"Hi, Lloyd," I say as I answer the phone, getting up and distancing myself as much as I possibly can from Mom. Her attention is already back on the TV.

On the other end, Lloyd makes an annoying *Mmmm* sound.

I rest my back against the sink, waiting for the other shoe to drop.

"Guess I'm kind of wondering where your loyalty lies, Sasha."

"I— What?" I clear my throat. "What do you mean? I've sent you everything I've gotten so far." It's true; I've emailed him about all my meet-ups with Rotten, hoping I had something he would approve for the story. Still, it doesn't stop the panic from spiking in my chest.

He sighs heavily. "Yeah, I'm just not feeling the angle on *'Rock Star Has Embarrassing High School Story Just Like All of Us'* for a breakout story. That's something he'd tell Jimmy So-and-so on a late-night show." Lloyd snorts at his own joke. "It's a little quirky that he's into rom-coms, but that's not a story. Do you want this scholarship or not?"

The thing is, as much as I want to hate Lloyd for being such a jerk, I know he's right.

"Understood." I take a deep breath. "Give me a little more time. I can dig up something good."

"I'll give you two weeks for a good pitch before I kill this offer."

Is it biologically possible for blood to turn cold?

Two weeks. I've only got two weeks to secure the rest of my future.

Even though he can't see me, I nod. Then, in a small voice, I say, "Okay. Thanks."

"We're all counting on you, S." He's never called me S before. No one does. "LA Now is a family. We're waiting for you to save the day."

"Okay," I say. "I get it."

"Yeah?" he asks, sounding a little more energetic.

"Yeah," I confirm. "I'm going to find something."

"That's my girl!" Lloyd's smiling now. I can hear it in his voice.

17

Daniel

We're working on what Silva calls the *finishing touches* for the album, but he's been saying that for the past two weeks. So I'm a little surprised when he gathers us in the studio after an extensive re-recording of drums from Wade that he wanted "just in case," and tells us, "We're almost there! Well done, everyone. Well done."

None of us responds immediately. Wade and Penny exchange a look. Sam's brows furrow. I guess I wasn't the only one feeling like we'd be in this studio re-recording the same tracks forever until we eventually withered away and died.

"When you say *almost there*," Penny says, "what do you mean exactly? How much work is left? Because I thought we were going to go over 'Instagram Zeitgeist' again. I'm not one hundred percent happy with the vocals there."

"Ouch," Wade jokes.

She gives him a small smile. "I mean mostly me. I can do better, especially in the chorus."

"Your singing is already perfect in it," I say. "But when you sing the bridge, I think the guitar is too loud. I was wondering if we could try to record it together, instead of doing it separately and then putting it together in the software. It might help with the tempo too," I say.

Everyone's looking at me like I've grown a second head.

"I think," I add.

Silva raises his eyebrows high. "I thought you were one of those mute kids."

"Silva, no." Wade shakes his head. "Not cool, man."

Silva shrugs. "I never heard his voice before."

Penny beams at me, a single dimple appearing in her right cheek. She tells me, "I actually think that's a really good idea, Rotten."

Mirroring her smile, I feel myself stand a little taller.

Sam puts a hand on my shoulder, and after a head-to-toe and toe-to-head look, he says, "That's a good point." Then he turns to Silva, hand still on my shoulder. "Maybe we could try playing that song all together to see how we like it, and then we can record it in whatever way you think will work better in postproduction."

Silva agrees. Everyone does.

"Before we start," Silva says, "I got an interesting invitation from a contact at Venice Beach." He raises his eyebrows. I feel like we all collectively hold our breaths. "How do you feel about a pop-up concert this weekend to promote the new album?"

"You said we're *practically* done, not done," Penny says.

She speaks before anyone else has the chance to, but I feel like we would all side with her.

It doesn't feel like we're ready. We're still feeling out the last details of the album. I still don't know if my song is going to make the album or not.

Silva's face falls.

"It does feel like it might be too soon," I offer in a small voice.

To my surprise, Sam says, "Are you sure? It sounds like a good opportunity to showcase the new material, give the fans a little teaser."

Penny looks at Wade. "What do you think?"

He shrugs. "I think Sam's right. I'd be happy to do it, but I don't want to rush into things if half the band doesn't think it's a good idea yet."

To defuse the tension, Silva clears his throat. "Well, let's stay focused on the album. We can talk about the pop-up concert later. You don't have to decide anything right now."

So we focus on what we know how to do. We play music.

The tips of my fingers are itching when I enter the glass case of the studio. Wade sits behind us all in the drums, Sam follows him closely, holding his bass, and Penny is the last to enter, pulling her braids up into a knot. She stretches, doing a short breathing exercise, while Silva prepares on the other side of the glass.

It's just me and the guitar now.

No tabloids, no paparazzi, just me and the instrument that gives me a voice.

Penny surprises me by looking up at me. She nods when I meet her eyes. Sam and Wade glance up at us too, and it's like we're all sharing something for just a moment.

"Instagram Zeitgeist" usually starts with an explosion of drums. But Wade holds back, and somehow I know what to do next.

I look at Wade, then at Sam, and back at Penny.

It's like we make an unspoken decision as a band, one that nobody would notice if they weren't watching closely. Wade's not going to start the song—I am.

My fingers strum the guitar once, then twice more. Penny grabs the mic, says, "One, two; one, two, three, go!" and Wade slams the tabs hard. I finally kick in with my part of the intro, and Sam follows me right along with the bass.

Penny screams the lyrics she wrote way back when we were still on the show. Sam bobs his head along to the bass, and I let loose enough to do the same. Our eyes meet, and we share the most electrifying moment: we're both completely lost in the music.

ROTTEN:

how's work?

SASHA:

i like how you always ask that

like waiting tables is going to have a sudden plot twist

:p

ROTTEN:

a good plot twist is one you don't see coming until it happens

maybe one day you'll answer that work's been chaotic

bc aliens came to visit

SASHA:

we shouldn't have netflix-partied that movie last night

ROTTEN:

i think it was a solid idea

SASHA:

you'll never let it go will you

it's really not that irrational to be afraid of aliens

they're from ANOTHER PLANET

it's SCARY, daniel

everyone's afraid of them!

I lean against the wall, waiting for the machine to reward me with fresh coffee, as I stare at my phone with what I'm sure are heart eyes.

Smiling, I send her a new text.

ROTTEN:

/i/ am not scared of aliens

SASHA:

this is why i don't trust you

I know she's joking.

But also . . . does she? Trust me?

I stare at her text.

She adds:

SASHA:

lol

The coffee machine beeps to warn me that the coffee is ready. When I look up from my phone, I see Penny entering the lounge. She waves a timid hello, then goes to the coffee machine as well.

I offer her my cup.

"Oh, thanks, but you drink espresso, right? Caffeine makes me too hyper. I just have some chocolate milk." She narrows her eyes, tilting her chin up. "Don't you dare laugh. Not everyone can be the bad boy of the band."

"I had no idea you knew what kind of coffee I had," I admit. "But yeah. Definitely not everyone can be a bad boy."

Penny selects her option on the machine and places her reusable green cup under the spout. I'm suddenly ashamed of my disposable plastic cup that's going to ruin the environment.

"Your feedback today was very cool," she says. "And playing together was great, right?"

She's not looking for confirmation, but it still feels good to nod.

"It's the most fun I've had in a while," she continues.

"Whoa, really?" I ask.

She scans me for sarcasm, and when she doesn't find it, she says, "I don't know why you're so surprised. We've all been stiff these last few weeks. I think it's because we're all so stressed with finishing the album already."

Penny sits on the big red puff against the wall, and I see that as an invitation to sit with her.

"Our album is really good. The critics are going to love it." I don't know why I say it, but she gives me a long and serious look.

Then she takes a sip of her chocolate milk and says, "I know we're good. But until our album comes out and the press loves it, the world still thinks we're just a reality-show band."

"Which we are," I offer. She glares playfully, and I add, "I know what you mean. I'm as excited as I am nervous. I want our music to be taken seriously."

Penny nods slowly. "Sam is making Wade lose his shit because he's so nervous. He might play it cool most of the time, but he's insecure. So Wade wants to strangle him, and I have to hear about it all night, every night."

"Oh . . ." I pause, freezing in my spot.

She gestures to my face. "What's that? That *oh*?"

I admit, "I didn't know you and Wade . . . were together."

"Mmmm," Penny starts, then shakes her head. "Now, there's a disgusting idea."

She looks like she's enjoying herself. My cheeks burn.

"You didn't know because there's nothing to know. I'm a lesbian, and plus, Wade's like a brother to me." She chuckles. "Nah, he just sleeps over most nights. His dad spends half his time in the US and half his time in Korea, and Wade doesn't like sleeping alone. Started coming over sometime around high school, and now he does it anytime he's stressed. My parents have known him forever, so they don't mind. He sleeps on the floor."

My phone beeps with a new text message, but I don't pick it up.

"I shouldn't have assumed. I didn't know you were gay," I say, but it sounds weird, so I try again. "I mean, I feel like I should have known, because I'm queer too. I'm demisexual."

She slowly points at the pin on her jacket. It's the lesbian flag. "Yeah, maybe you should have figured it out by now."

Though I'm embarrassed to have never paid attention to that, we end up both laughing. She shakes her head, then laughs some more. My cheeks still burn, but we stay sitting side by side, finishing our drinks.

"Maybe you just spent too long looking inward. You could've looked out. We could've been friends for longer," Penny says.

I just nod, looking down.

Maybe because she senses my tension, she asks, like an afterthought, "Hey, not that it's any of my business either, but how does being demi *and* a player work? How do you have the emotional bandwidth to juggle all that?"

I take a deep breath and steady myself. If I'm ever going to be honest with my bandmates, I have to start now.

"I don't. And I'm not. Sasha is my first girlfriend, and I don't even know if she sees it that way, because we haven't even kissed yet."

Penny kisses her teeth. "Shit."

I nod. "Shit."

My phone beeps again.

"Then you should probably get that," Penny says, and points at my phone. "And maybe ask her where you two stand. Tell her how you feel. All that good stuff."

SASHA:

i was kidding btw

okaaaay now you're making it seem like you were abducted when we were just talking about aliens. nothing sus about that

I smile at the text. Then at Penny, who's still looking at her empty cup like she's processing our conversation.

"I think we should say yes to Silva," Penny says. When she sees my blank look, she adds, "What he told us before. About the pop-up concert on Venice Beach."

I hold my breath.

"You thought it was too soon."

She nods. "I know. But the boys were right. We'll be teasing the new album for the first time, testing the waters. . . . It could be really good publicity. I just said that because I was scared. But I don't want to be scared. I want us to be big." She pauses. "That is, if that's something you'd be interested in."

Excitement bubbles up in my chest. "I know what you mean. I'm scared too. But maybe that's a good thing."

"Does that mean you want to do it?" She grins.

I nod, slowly at first, then for real. "Yeah. I suppose so."

A pop-up concert. Just like that.

I feel like I'm smiling harder than the Joker, but I can't help the butterflies in my stomach. It'll be our first time playing in public since being on *Making Music!*

And Sasha will be there to see it too.

18

Sasha

Tomorrow's my last shot.

I'm standing in front of Claire as she takes off her Angeles Diner apron. She's staring at me suspiciously, like she can see the gears turning in my head.

"Is everything with your mom okay?"

I frown. "Um, yes? She's fine."

Claire nods, turning to get her purse from her locker in the small staff room. "So if your mom's okay, then I guess something must've happened on the Rotten front. You look weird, so don't try to deny it. *Something's* going on with you."

How the heck does she know these things? I'm glad she can't see my face right now. "He just texted me, actually. Invited me—I mean, *us* technically—to a pop-up concert. It's tomorrow."

Claire gasps, spins around, and grabs my shoulders in disbelief. "OhmyGodareyouforreal? I'm going to a Mischief and Mayhem gig, and you tell me like *this*? Why did you not prepare me? Oh man, I feel like I'm going to pass out! Why are you not passing out? Why are you sulking? *Sasha!* Where's the concert?"

That pulls me out of my own world, where I'm thinking about the fact that I have to nail this piece once and for all. I blink a few times, feigning a smile. "Venice Beach. Can you borrow your mom's car?"

"Sasha, that's the *least* of my concerns. My biggest one being *what will we wear?!*"

"Not this, I hope," I say, pointing at my own apron.

Her eyes sparkle. "We need to go shopping!"

The idea of going shopping in my spare time feels like torture, but I do want to look my best.

After all, it's going to be my chance. For what, exactly, I'm not sure. Hopefully for burying the butterflies in my stomach for real and focusing on the plan ahead.

For a Los Angeles resident, I don't actually enjoy going to the beach that much. The ocean? Yes. I love watching it and listening to the waves, which is part of why Sunken City is my favorite place. But going to the beach as an activity, dressed in a bikini and surrounded by hundreds of loud people, is not my idea of a good time necessarily.

But Claire has prepared me for this. We both got mani-pedis—my toes and fingers are now a cute shade of pastel pink—and I'm wearing a new bikini that she bought for me as a birthday gift, even though my birthday is in December. My bikini is cotton-candy pink, and while I wouldn't have picked out the color myself, I have to agree with Claire that it looks pretty good against my brown skin. I'm wearing a lightweight dress on top, the same linen one that I wore to Rotten's pool party. My hair is pulled into low pigtails, my short hair barely staying in the hair bands, but it looks cute and fun.

I look cute and fun.

I'm not sure I'd use these words to describe myself in general, but today I am. I feel awesome.

Claire's wearing a new, dark green one-piece, with her straight hair styled into a single braid. And she's wearing a see-through orange dress that makes the ensemble look like a million dollars. She's also carrying a ridiculous clear plastic bag with just her keys, wallet, and phone—the only kind of bag they'll let us bring into the concert. It kind of looks awful, but I offered to carry it so I could have my phone handy in case Daniel decides to come downstage and talk to me.

I don't know what I was thinking. Of course he won't—he and I aren't public or anything. I've been lucky that nobody's identified me in the blurry pictures people have taken of us, but I know he wouldn't risk my privacy by singling me out in an event like this.

Look at me, thinking about what *Rotten* would and wouldn't do for me. . . .

I blink. It's impossible to think of him as Rotten now that I know him as Daniel.

Claire spreads her arms toward the ocean and takes an exaggerated breath. "We're here," she says. "Can you believe it?" I've been mostly focusing on the sand making its way into my flip-flops, but her excitement makes me glad she's here, glad *I'm* here. Venice Beach isn't my top favorite location in Los Angeles, but it's all right. The tall palm trees give us a little shade, the sand is white, and the sea's inviting.

"Let's dip our toes in the water," Claire suggests, giving me a wide-eyed look, like she has just suggested going skinny-dipping or something. They're still putting the stage together, so I smile at her and take off toward the water.

I grip the plastic purse a little closer to my chest, my flip-flops in the other hand, as I walk toward the ocean. It's calmer today than most days. Still a little windy, but the sun's high enough in the bright afternoon sky that it doesn't matter. Still feels warm. Still smells like summer.

Claire runs into the water and kicks a wave up to the sky with a joyous shriek.

People look. She doesn't seem to care.

I take my time, inching in until the water's up to my ankles, and I watch my toes very slowly disappear into the sand. I move them around, a little smile playing in the corner of my mouth, and they disappear again.

The smell of summer is salt and ocean, sand and sun. I don't know how all of this somehow became ordinary to me over the years, but I guess that's what happens when you live in the place other people go to for vacation.

Behind us, people are starting to gather for the concert. Claire told me there were some rumors online that Mischief & Mayhem would be performing a pop-up gig today, but no one knew the location yet. With the commotion of black-T-shirted staff setting up a stage in Venice Beach, my guess is that it won't be long before more fans start showing up.

On our way in, we heard a curious middle-aged couple asking a staff member about the concert. The staffer said they don't know who's performing. I'm not sure I buy it, but I appreciate the mystery.

The band should be here within the next hour.

The stage is pretty small for a band like them. Once they take the stage, their band name written in colossal letters behind Wade and his drums, it's clear that they're larger than life. Penny grabs the microphone and says, "Good evening, Venice Beach. We are Mischief and Mayhem, and we're here to *rock*."

Immediately there's a shift in the atmosphere.

Wade's white hair contrasts against his dark roots behind the drums. Closest to him, Sam is wearing black skinny jeans, his red bass slung over his shoulder. Penny has long pink locs and a mermaid-green short dress over a white bikini top.

And to her left, there's Daniel, squinting and scanning the crowd . . .

For me.

Daniel with his messy dark hair and white electric guitar, looking serious and otherworldly, not smiling for the crowd, not because he thinks he's too good for everyone but because he's too shy to hold anyone's eye. He's wearing ripped blue jeans with a loose black shirt, so oversized that I can see his rib cage when he turns to Penny to whisper something.

Penny grins, and they all exchange a look.

"This is a new song, so we hope you like it. It's called 'Interlude to Salvation.' Let's go!" she screams, and immediately Wade slams the drums.

Penny starts singing, taking the mic off its stand and walking around the stage as if challenging the whole beach to have as much fun as she is.

They are infectiously energetic and beautiful, and everyone's entranced.

The high notes of the guitar and low notes of the bass have a rippling effect on the crowd. People start dancing, jumping, and cheering loudly. It's mostly people around our age and younger, but there are also older folks who are probably not the band's core demographic. People who were with their families at the beach bob their heads from afar or join the crowd in front of the stage.

And as Daniel shreds the guitar, his eyes finally find mine.

I feel like I'm the center of his world, and *that* makes me weak in the knees.

I beam at him.

Beside me, Claire laughs. "Say 'cheese'!"

. . . What?

I turn to her, frowning, but she's already looking at the photo she took of me on her phone. I'm not a fan of having my picture taken, especially not when I'm swooning over a guy. And I definitely don't want there to be a photo of me at a Mischief & Mayhem concert when the tabloids have been posting blurry photos of my face every time I go out with Daniel. It's only a matter of time before someone makes the connection, figures out who I am.

But I'm not going to let this ruin my day.

"Put your phone away and let's get closer to the stage! I want to dance," I instruct.

She nods, saying, "Yes, boss!" but still thumbs away at her phone for another moment.

I roll my eyes. Holding hands, we're pulled forward by the magnetism that is their music.

It's not perfect, but also it kind of is.

We dance our hearts out to two songs before I realize my phone's blowing up with notifications in the see-through purse. The only people who ever message me are Claire, who's right beside me, or Mom, so I pull Claire away from the crowd and take my phone out, a frown already clouding my face.

"What's up?" she asks.

The notifications aren't from text messages. They're from Instagram. People following me, tagging me, replying to my latest picture. I go to my picture, one I took of the sunset in Sunken City—not with Daniel but before summer break. It's just a picture of the ocean, but people are calling me names, accusing me of stealing their boyfriend.

My stomach sinks, and a disgusting taste crawls up my throat. My fingers are shaky when I click out of the picture and scroll through my notifications.

Claire is still dancing to the music off to the side, not paying any attention to me.

But I can't stop staring at her after I see what caused this flood of messages.

It's the picture she took of me, staring at Daniel. He's in the background, staring right back at me, and I swear, it's like you can see the hearts in our eyes.

Claire tagged me in it, but she also tagged a Mischief & Mayhem fan account. The first comment, the one with the most likes, is from a popular fan account. They've included a screenshot of Rotten carrying me in his arms after the pool party, writing:

SO *THAT'S* ROTTEN'S SECRET GIRLFRIEND????

I feel like I might throw up.

"Claire!" I shout above the music. "Claire!" I tug on her arm, pull her back to reality.

She's still smiling as she turns to look at me, and I watch the smile fade with the same sense of dread that I feel every time my phone lights up with another notification.

"Did something happen?" she asks, her brows furrowing.

I shove the phone at her face, and she takes a step back. "I . . . *Wow.*"

"*Wow?*" I say. "What do you mean, *wow*? What did you do?"

Her eyes go wide. "Listen, I'm so sorry. I didn't know this was going to happen. I only meant—"

"What did you *think* was gonna happen?" I shout.

A few people look at us, but they're more interested in the concert than two random girls who are clearly in the middle of an epic fight.

They probably haven't seen the picture. Probably don't know that it feels like something inside me is breaking.

"I'm sorry they're coming after you!" Claire says. "It's just, so many people were talking shit online about how Rotten was dating this actress that I bet he doesn't even know—" She rolls her eyes. My eyebrows shoot up, equal parts outraged and disappointed. She sees my expression and continues in a rush. "I wanted to show everyone that they were wrong! That's *all*. I didn't even mean to tag you.

It was muscle memory—I tag you in every picture I take with you!"

I take another step back, my face blank.

"No, please," she says, holding out her hands to me, like she wants me to grab hold of them, like we did when we first walked down the beach. "I'm sorry I tagged you. I'll untag you. Okay? I'll do it now." She rushes to get her phone.

As if that would make a difference now.

I'll have to lock down all my social media. Maybe delete my accounts. I don't know.

"You sold me out because you were annoyed? What, you wanted to prove that you're their biggest fan or something?" I ask, but I'm not really asking. I'm just saying it out loud to sound out the words.

Claire shakes her head, and tears fill her eyes. In the back of my mind, I know she wasn't necessarily trying to hurt me. She's impulsive, never thinks twice before doing something, and maybe it's true that she didn't tag me on purpose, and that she didn't even consider the consequences of revealing my identity.

But what she meant is irrelevant. What she did outweighs her intention.

My phone keeps beeping.

"Sasha, please," she begs.

"I'm going to take a bus home." I turn away from her, tears burning my eyes too.

She grabs my wrist and tries to stop me, but I yank it

away. I glare at her in a way that makes her recoil. In the background, Penny's singing about how nothing can ruin tonight. I'm thinking she's wrong.

My hands are shaking by the time I get to the bus stop. I unlock my phone, planning to lock all my social accounts, but first I see a text from my boss.

LLOYD:

Just saw the most interesting thing online.

What the fuck? Your name's out there

I advise you to write the piece now before somcone gets the scoop on YOU

19

Daniel

I feel like I'm flying. In the back of my mind I'm still worried about the way the M&M fans attacked Sasha yesterday when her Instagram profile leaked. I was upset, but it was hard to *stay* upset when the pop-up gig turned out to be such a success. So many people showed up midconcert, like they'd heard of it and stopped whatever they were doing to come straight to Venice Beach. Our agent, Bobbi, emailed us a few positive headlines from articles about the concert that have already been posted, but she said there is sure to be more press coming.

People seemed to like our songs. And they only got a teaser of what our album's going to be.

Yesterday may have been a big win, but today is somehow even better.

Because we finally finished the album.

It's Penny who gives me a high five while Wade and Sam embrace. Then Sam steps away from their hug, like he's embarrassed at how emotional he's being. Wade, on the other hand, is tearing up, not at all afraid to show his feelings.

"I think this is the second-happiest day of my life," he admits.

"Is the first when we got to the finals of *Making Music!*?" I ask him, giving him a hug too.

He rests his head on my shoulder a moment, too tall for our embrace, and turns to Penny. "Nah. The best day of my life was my sixteenth birthday. First car." He pulls away, giving Penny a meaningful look.

Moments like this, when their shared history bubbles to the surface, still happen. But I don't feel as alienated now. Penny rolls her eyes and gives him a playful shove, and then they hug properly. She holds his face and brushes his tears away, and then Sam is giving me a hug too.

"We did it. Can you believe?" He smiles, big and genuine. "We finished recording the album!"

I've never seen Sam so happy. It's kind of strange. And awesome.

We're standing in the lounge on the eighteenth floor of our music label's building, exchanging looks with each other like we're giddy children, when Penny whips out her phone and says, "Party! We need to celebrate. I know someone who owns this awesome club. Hold on, let me see if they still have a VIP booth for tonight."

Wade throws himself onto the L-shaped couch, wiping the remaining tears from his eyes, and when Sam joins him, there's a mischievous smile on Sam's face. Pun not intended.

"So all tracks are in place *except* for the final track." Sam raises his eyebrows, playful. "Invite Sasha to our party tonight. We have to decide if she's really into you . . . and if she is, you win."

I chuckle dryly, feeling like I'm finally hitting the drop after coming all the way to the top of the roller coaster.

Sam being the judge of whether Sasha likes me? That doesn't sound like flying.

Penny looks up from her phone. "What did you just say?"

Sam grins sheepishly. "We made a bet in the beginning of summer," he explains. "It's about 'Inconsequence.'"

"The song we wrote?" Judging by her look, she already knows the answer. Still I nod, and Sam explains the rest of the bet. She gives both of us blank eyes when he's done talking. "So instead of resolving this like the two adults you almost are and bringing it up in a band meeting so we could vote on the song, you decided to make a bet on an innocent girl's heart?"

Her question is directed at Sam, but I answer. "It's not like that. Sam just bet that I couldn't stay with her all summer."

Penny stares at me. Then she points at Wade. "You let that happen?"

"I thought it was romantic." Wade shrugs.

She rolls her eyes. "This is so ridiculous."

"I thought you might say that," Sam declares. "That's why you weren't in on the bet, because you're no fun." Penny briefly gives him the middle finger, then turns her attention back to her phone. "But I meant it! We have to decide who won the bet tonight. Silva will need the list with the songs and the order of the tracks by tomorrow morning anyway."

I take a deep breath.

"We're in," Penny says, looking up at us again. "For the VIP booth at the club, I mean. Tonight we're partying!"

There's no going back now. And I'm feeling pretty good about my chances of winning.

"I'll invite Sasha," I say.

DANIEL:

How are you?

SASHA:

I had to beg my mom to not fight trolls so I don't look pathetic

So there's that

DANIEL:

Won't you PLEASE just let me tell people to leave you alone?

SASHA:

That's gonna make things worse

Trust me

The less attention drawn to myself, the better

People will just forget

Eventually

DANIEL:

It helps if something else happens to distract them, right?

SASHA:

Yes . . . ?

DANIEL:

We finished recording the album:)

Hoping they'll leave you alone and focus on that

SASHA:

AHHHH!!!!! OMG!!!!
THIS IS EXCELLENT!!!
CONGRATULATIONS!!!!!!!

[catparty.gif]

DANIEL:

:)))) I'll text you the address of the wrap party!

If you want to come ofc

SASHA:

Would never miss it ;)

This place is scary-big. It's a club hidden in a residential area, in a duplex apartment with a view of the skyline. Not that I've seen much of the skyline. Between the dry ice fogging up the dance floor and the neon lights flashing while the music blasts, I haven't seen much of anything.

The VIP area is set off from the dance floor, enough that you can actually maintain a conversation over the thumping beats. Past the security guards, there are booths with loose curtains around each of them, in the same tacky, dark red theme. I counted six VIP booths on this side, elevated off the ground a few feet. Waiters with trays of drinks drift toward the tables.

I'm on my third Monster can, and I don't even like energy drinks.

Sam lowers his head so he's eye level with me in the booth and asks, "Are you okay, dude?"

He's smiling, like he thinks my nerves are hilarious.

"I'm fine," I say, feigning confidence.

Sasha should be here any moment.

Wade beams at me from behind Sam. Sam says, "I think you're going to unscrew your leg from your groin. Stop that." He holds my knee still, forcing me to stop bouncing it up and down. "Much better."

Beside me, Penny sighs. "Stop bullying our local 'bad boy,' children."

Sam and Wade both leave to go back to the dance floor, or to the bar, or wherever they're planning on spending the rest of their night, and I turn to Penny. "Thank you. I think. You did sound very ironic calling me a bad boy just now."

She's wearing her locs in two pigtails. She looks down at

her nails, painted a soft brown. "Um, no. I'm just wondering about the outcome of tonight. If you'll finally tell Sasha how you feel."

I tense up. "The bet is about how *she* feels, I think. Like, if we look like a real couple, or—"

"I truly could not give less of a damn about your dumb bet, Rotten."

The way she says it, her mouth curled into a smirk, makes me think she knows something I don't. Or something I've known from day one but have been trying not to think about. That she's not the only one who doesn't care about the bet . . .

I care about the song. I care about it making the album.

But I care about Sasha so much more.

I want this to be real, 100 percent.

Then I see her across the room, like an actual slow-motion entrance in a movie.

I don't care that the song playing is a senseless techno beat, because in my head, it's a soft rock ballad. Full-on guitars with bass and drums, melody with no lyrics, because we don't need words.

Sasha walks around the perimeter of the dance floor, searching the crowd with her eyes. For *me.* She's wearing a sleeveless, metallic-green dress with a heart-shaped cutout, exposing her collarbones. She looks gorgeous.

My throat dries.

"Go get her," Penny says.

My heart feels like it's going to jump out of my chest. "I—I will."

I get up and wave at her until she sees me.

She beams.

My chest. Might. Explode.

I meet her halfway through the VIP area, and she stops in front of me, almost shy. I've never thought of her that way. She tucks a strand of hair behind her ear. "Hey."

"Hey," I say. *You look beautiful. You* are *beautiful.*

I don't know why I don't say these things.

"Wanna dance?" I ask.

She grins. "Y—"

"I'm not actually good," I say, interrupting her. "And um, you just got here. Don't you wanna sit first, maybe get something to drink? Do you like energy drinks? Or something else. I'm not judging. Do you want to sit?"

Sasha laughs and takes my hand. "Let's dance, Daniel."

My hand burns at her touch. And it feels really, really good, to have her say my name, to have her fingers intertwining with mine as she guides me to the dance floor as if this is her scene.

Dancing with Sasha is the most intoxicating experience I've had, and I just finished recording my debut album.

It doesn't matter that I can't dance. It doesn't matter that I don't like the music. All that matters is that her body is close to mine. All that matters is that her forehead touches my shoulder every now and then, and when she takes a step back, she smirks up at me.

My hands slide down her exposed back as we dance, and they nearly tremble.

Maybe they do.

Too much energy drink. Or too much Sasha. I'm definitely high on *something.*

As I pull her closer, and closer still, we move to the music.

It's like my heart is on fire.

And it feels so good.

We dance for two songs before she pulls away from me with a sparkle in her eye. "I need to go to the restroom. Meet you back at your booth?"

"Okay," I say. Then, before she turns away, she does something unexpected.

She gets on her tiptoes and presses a kiss onto my cheek.

I don't dodge her this time. All I want to do is turn so she'll kiss me on the lips instead.

But I stay planted, my head spinning. The feeling of her hands on my biceps and her lips on my cheek lingers after she gives me a small wave. I watch her disappear in the crowd, and I feel like today might be the happiest day of my life, for more than one reason.

I go back to our booth and find my friends making bizarre (Wade) and rather obscene (Sam) gestures. I roll my eyes, sitting down between Penny and Wade. Sam, on Wade's other side, reaches across our drummer to pat me on the thigh.

"Are you ready for our bet assessment?" he asks.

"*Love* assessment," Wade says, correcting him. His speech is already a little slurred.

Sam waves him away. "It's with much pain in my heart that I declare that the winner is . . ."

Penny raises her eyebrows. "If you're also competing, how come you get to announce who the winner is? That's shady."

Sam ignores her. "*You!* Rotten, I have to say, I hate losing, but Sasha is definitely into you. You did it. You won the bet, my man."

It's weird having him call me *my man,* but not weirder than the rush of adrenaline I feel when I hear these words. "Inconsequence" is going to make it to the album. The song I had a hand in writing. The song that means so much to me.

"So the song—?" I start, just to make sure.

"Obviously," Penny replies. "Again, I'd just like to note that we could've discussed this as professionals instead of doing all this. But I digress."

Wade slaps my shoulder, wearing a huge grin. "You won more than the track. You won *love*!"

My face is burning at his cheesy remark. But I'm smiling.

This level of support is new. Winning at anything feels like it's new too.

"Let's toast!" Sam announces, and starts filling glasses of champagne that I won't drink.

Beside me, Penny says quietly, "Watching the two of you, it's obvious that you two belong together. It's really cute. But . . . you have to tell her how you feel, you know."

I nod. I fully plan on doing that.

When Sasha finally finds me again, Penny has disappeared somewhere on the dance floor, and Sam and Wade are leaving the VIP area to get the numbers of some models who are, according to both of them, *super hot*.

"Hey," she says. "Sorry about that. Miss me?"

"Of course I did," I say. Taking a leap of faith, I touch her forearm, my eyes attentive to her reaction. They dance between her skin and her eyes, asking for permission as my hand slides down her arm all the way to the palm of her hand. She doesn't say anything until my fingers find hers.

They interlace, fitting well together.

"So . . . Penny's friends with the owner of this club," I say.

"Well connected," she says, mocking, but I can tell her heart's not in it. She's still staring at our hands.

"She gave me the keys to the rooftop," I explain. "Wanna go?"

This is the second leap. If she lets me, there's a third one coming.

She glances around, like she's trying to find something. She swallows hard, looking at me with a resolve I haven't seen before.

"Yeah." She squeezes my hand. "Let's go."

We hold hands every step of the way. Even when going up the stairs, and it would be more comfortable to let go. I finally let go to unlock the door to the roof; she's quiet beside me, and I wish I could ask what's on her mind. Instead I push open the door and walk into the open area.

I'm nervous, so I state the obvious: "It's a starry night."

"Whoa," she breathes out, walking behind me.

It is stunning. The glittery skyline surrounds us, like each light below is a fallen star, but the real spectacle is in the sky. The night is kind to us, shining bright and clear. There's nothing on the rooftop other than TV antennas, but it still feels like a special place. You can't even hear the techno music from here.

Sasha's eyes are bright as she gets closer to the edge, resting her elbows on the wall, looking up with her mouth agape. I lick my lips, pushing down thoughts that are probably not super appropriate, and stand next to her.

"I've been wanting to tell you something." I clear my throat, looking down instead of up. There's nothing nice to see down. Parked cars, some trees. Other buildings. "That day back at my place, the pool party?"

Sasha chuckles. She bumps her elbow against mine playfully. "Please don't mention the most embarrassing moment of my life."

I shake my head. "I just . . . I didn't know if I wanted to kiss you yet."

This earns me a glare. "Ouch?" She raises her eyebrows. "Okay. I mean, that much was clear, but to hear you say it—"

"Listen, it's not like that." I take a deep breath, turning so my back is resting against the wall and I can look at her properly. I'm a tiny bit terrified it won't make sense to her, but I press on. "It takes me a little while longer, you know? For me, it's not . . . looking at people and finding them attractive, if that makes sense? I know they're gorgeous, but I'm not necessarily attracted, until . . ."

But she pushes. "Until?"

My throat is dry.

"Until something happens," I say. "Something clicks inside me."

She's quiet for a second; then the corner of her mouth goes up.

"Sorry. I don't want this to sound— I'm not proposing, by the way— I'm trying to say that it wasn't you. I needed more time." She watches me closely. "I've had time. And, Sasha, I'm not sure how to say this without sounding a little intense, but I'm *so* attracted to you."

Sasha sighs. "Oh, thank God."

"What?" I laugh.

"Because, I mean, I am too," she explains. "I was really hoping this was going in a direction where you were going to kiss me, because I very much want to kiss you, Daniel."

She beams at me, challenging and waiting at the same time.

"Come here," I say.

Then I place my hand on the side of her face, my body burning and my chest tight. She leans closer, her hands wrapping in my shirt, like this has taken oh-so-long. Our foreheads touch, eyes meeting for another second.

Time for the third leap.

I kiss her.

20

Sasha

I'm so into this guy that I'm angry with myself.

His hands are on my face and the back of my neck, and I can't get enough of him. I arch my body against him, kissing him back, tasting the energy drink and chasing his shyness away, my hands still clasped on his shirt.

I pull back for air, feeling my breath hot against his, our faces still touching. "I get it. I really do," I say.

"What's that?" he asks, but he doesn't sound particularly curious.

He kisses my cheek, then the corner of my mouth. His hands slide down my back, keeping me close. I'm glad he's holding me, because my legs might have turned to jelly a tiny little bit.

I chuckle, leaning into him, letting him steal another kiss before I speak again.

"Why you get all the girls."

"What girls?" he asks, like it's a reflex.

"You know." I let go of his shirt, even though I don't feel very dismissive about it. "All the models and the actresses and stuff. All the girls you've hooked up with. I'm not—I'm not judging," I say, judging. "I get it."

Rotten—no, not Rotten.

He asked me to call him Daniel. Does he ask everyone to call him that?

It doesn't matter. I've made up my mind.

Daniel.

Daniel's hand comes up to hold my face, like I'm the most precious thing.

"That's what I've been wanting to tell you," he says. "There's only you. You're my first kiss."

I blink slowly.

"This was my first kiss, I mean," Daniel adds.

"I'm not sure I . . . I follow."

Daniel murmurs, "Right," and then takes my hand again. He sits down, and invites me to sit with him.

I clench my purse tighter. Suddenly I'm feeling a little funny.

He takes a deep breath, still holding my hand. His hand is calloused from playing the guitar, and is way too big in mine, and I like that. I'm taken by an almost impossible desire to kiss his hand.

Instead I sit very still.

"That can't possibly have been your first kiss," I state matter-of-factly.

"I'm telling you the truth," he says. "I've never gotten

that far with anyone." He clears his throat, but then doesn't say anything else.

I frown, staring at him.

"I want to believe you, but—"

"Then believe me."

His eyes are so sincere. Oh my God, they really are. I'm stunned by the truth in them. My fear of believing him isn't big enough to drown out the happiness I feel in this moment.

"So the player rumors are fake. What else isn't true?"

Daniel considers this. "You may have heard that I'm this wild party animal. The tabloids like to think so."

"And you're not?"

"Never had a drink in my life, much less drugs."

I raise my eyebrows. "Never?"

He nods. "Never even one drink."

"So the player rumors are fake, and you don't drink. And you're friends with your sister, and you're a rom-com aficionado, and I was your first kiss." I breathe out, after saying it all in one go. He chuckles, still looking at our hands. "Am I missing anything?"

"That I crochet when I'm anxious," he says.

Daniel sneaks a peek at me, like he wants to check my reaction.

I'm feeling a million of things at once.

From fear in the pit of my stomach that he may be lying, to a weird lightheartedness that tells me to believe him.

I've already taken the plunge and decided to believe in this relationship.

"I'm not much of a rock star," he admits.

Well, I think he's wonderful.

I can't find the words.

So I set my purse aside and kiss him instead, hoping I can communicate what I think through my actions. Because the truth is that I feel so much. And he holds me for dear life, like I'm everything.

In that moment, all there is, is *us.* I don't even remember my purse, lying on the roof, with the recorder that caught our whole conversation still turned on.

21

Daniel

It's the best day of my life.

No, it's going to be the best *week* of my life. And month and year.

I can't remember the last time I crocheted not because I was anxious and needed to do something with my hands but because I was *happy*. I've gotten halfway through a scarf that I'm going to give to Helena, when my phone buzzes. It's still way too early to be a bandmate, or even Sasha, so I don't really make an effort to get out of bed.

Smiling to myself, I let go of the needle in the middle of a stitch, my other hand still wrapped around wool as I rest them on my stomach, closing my eyes and lying back on the bed. What a wonderful night.

I haven't been able to fall asleep since I left Sasha at her place. I made her a promise to take her out today. We're going to the Santa Monica Pier, which she assures me is too touristy, but I'll make sure we have the best date. I've already thought about all the songs we should listen to on the way there.

I look at the guitars on the wall, remembering how surreal it was to buy enough guitars that I can use them as decor. I consider picking up one of my actual guitars—my favorite acoustic one—from its stand, but it's not even seven in the morning yet, and I don't want to wake up Helena.

Instead I'm going to browse through all my streaming services and make a list of the romantic comedy classics I want to introduce to Sasha. She'll definitely fall in love with the genre. I'm biting back a smile as I yawn. Then my phone buzzes again, insistent.

I grab my phone from the floor where it's charging. I turn the screen toward me, and . . . It's Dad. Dad's calling. It takes me a moment, recognizing the word *PAI* on the screen. He never, ever calls.

Squatting, with a frown on my face, I hesitantly slide my finger over the screen to take the call.

"Finally," he says in Portuguese. "I thought you wouldn't pick it up, Daniel. Where were you?"

I get my shyness from my dad. He never yells, never sounds stressed, never speaks as if someone's life is on the line. Never sounds like this.

I clear my throat, sitting down on the floor. "Pai, oi," I say. "Sorry, I was . . . I was taking a shower, and then . . . I was— What happened? Is everything okay? Is Mom okay?"

Dad sighs heavily. I can hear faraway voices through the phone.

"Where are you?" I ask.

Don't say what I think you'll say. Don't say what I think you'll say. Don't—

"We're in the hospital," he says.

Time freezes.

My first kiss, the club, Sasha, it feels like it was all light-years ago. I feel sick.

"Pai," I repeat, but I don't recognize my voice.

"I don't get how this happened, because your mother never misses her medication—"

My voice comes thicker this time, more demanding, but more fragile too. *"No."*

"It was a heart attack. That's what they're *saying,* at least." He spits out the last sentence, like he knows more than the doctors.

"No. She can't . . ." I close my eyes, willing this conversation to go away.

Dad doesn't speak. I want to cry. I want Mom to hug me. I want to know that she's fine.

She has to be fine.

"Are you alone?" I ask, feeling like a child again, several countries away and scared.

"No, your aunt's here. She went looking for the doctor; this hospital is a mess." Dad makes a disappointed noise. "Daniel, I don't understand. She always takes her heart medication. . . ."

I don't want to hear this anymore. Not from him. I need to hear Mom's voice telling me that *of course* she is well.

"I'll call you when we know more. I have to go now. Tell your sister, okay?" he asks.

Sure. If he talked directly to Helena, she might demand answers and do *something* instead of sitting on the floor, eyes welling up, feeling like everything is falling apart.

He hangs up before I agree.

I hold the phone in my hands, staring at it like it's cursed.

Before I know what's happening, I'm sobbing.

Helena and I share her bed like we used to when we were little kids. Our parents would go out, and we would stay in her bed, watching her favorite rom-coms, while she talked about older people I didn't know. Sometimes we would listen to her favorite albums.

Our grandfather died when I was eight and she was thirteen. I wasn't allowed to go to the funeral because I was too young, but Helena went. When she came back, I was under the covers in her bedroom, waiting for her. She slipped under the covers with me, and we cried together. I don't remember anything else from that night, and barely anything else from that year.

Now I'm seventeen and she's twenty-two, and while I'm sitting cross-legged by the end of her bed, she's sitting at the other end, pressed against the back of her bed, hugging her knees, while she talks to our dad on her cell. Her hair is pulled into a bun; her eyes and nose are red from crying. I look at her over my shoulder, sniffing, trying to deal with my own red eyes and nose.

"Right," she says to the phone, sounding annoyed. "I learned about this in school, Pai. It's common knowledge. Women don't always suffer the same symptoms as men with heart attacks." Pause. Dry chuckle. "You should *know* that. Especially since Mom's a chain-smoker."

"Stop being mean," I tell her, but she ignores me.

"Of course it's your responsibility. Mom's older than you. And you're her husband." As her voice grows louder, she grows smaller. I watch my sister shrink, hugging herself closer and closer.

I take a deep breath and reach for Helena's foot across the bed. I touch her ankle, trying to anchor her back. She snaps her head up. "He's suffering too. Try to be understanding," I say, trying to keep my voice as clear as possible.

Helena rolls her eyes and shoves the phone in my direction.

Sighing, I let her go and take the phone.

"Hi, Dad. It's Daniel again."

On the other end, Dad's crying. "How was I supposed to know your mom was having a heart attack? I swear to God, I hope Helena never has to find out what it feels like to be afraid like this. I thought I was going to lose your mother."

Helena buries her face in her knees.

I breathe out heavily.

"But she's going to be okay, right?"

"They're still doing exams," he says. "I don't know, Daniel. Okay? I don't know."

"I'm sorry we're not there with you," I say, and I don't think I've ever meant it as much as I mean it now.

Not last Christmas or the missed birthdays or on the random days when it felt like I couldn't make it in a new country. Now I mean it. Now I want to be there with them, and most important, with Mom.

"I miss you. I miss you two so much," Dad says. My aunt says something on the other end, and he cries again. "Okay, I . . . we have to go. Take care of each other, okay? Eu amo vocês."

"Também te amo."

After I hang up Helena's phone, I look at her. Tears are running freely down her face, and I feel so damn guilty. The only reason she's here is because of me. I took her away from our family. The only reason we're both away is me.

I crawl under the blanket with her. I can't even say I'm sorry.

All I have is an impossible weight pressing down on my chest, and Dad's voice in my ear, telling me he doesn't know if Mom's going to be all right.

22

Sasha

Vanessa blows a pink bubble until it explodes, shattering the silence in the LA Now office.

"You look happier than usual," she states, like I'm suddenly very interesting.

I'm smiling from ear to ear. Of course I'm happier than usual.

Nonchalant, I shrug.

Vanessa chuckles. "It's the teen has-been in the making, isn't it?" she teases. I glare at her, and she shoots her hands up in a sign of peace. "I don't listen to rock. I don't care about his name. My one true love is Britney Spears."

Biting back a smile, I tell her, "*Daniel.* His name is Daniel. But he goes by *Rotten* in the press."

Not that I'd admit this, but saying his name—his *real* name—out loud makes me feel some kind of way. I'm not the press. I'm something else.

I might even be his girlfriend.

God. What a thought. What a feeling.

Am I . . . giggling?

I turn my face away so Vanessa won't make fun of me.

But she's just giving me a look, like she's not sure what to make of this.

I clear my throat to compose myself. No giggling. I'm here as a semi-professional. I'm here with my portfolio and my printed exclusive, hoping this is the story that puts me in Lloyd's good scholarship graces.

As if on cue, Vanessa's desk phone rings. She gestures for me to wait. After a few hums of acknowledgment and okays, she hangs up and tells me, "Lloyd's ready to see you, Sasha."

I take a deep breath and get up from the chair.

"Okay. Thank you."

"Good luck," she adds, with a slight frown.

My heart beats faster with each step. By the time I finally knock on Lloyd's door, my knuckles are trembling. When he yells for me to come in, I feel completely out of my element.

"Afternoon, Sasha." He greets the papers in my hands instead of me, eyes on them already. It must take everything in him not to jump on them and completely ignore me. "Sit, sit."

So I sit.

"Hi, Lloyd," I begin. "I'm here on a Saturday instead of emailing you because—"

"Sensitive information. Of course." He glances at my face very briefly, then back at the papers. "Can I see? Unless you want to pitch me the story first?"

Yesterday I felt so sure about this plan—my *new* plan. And I *know* it's a good story. I have the audio to use as proof if we're sued for defamation. I have video clips. I have enough photographs for a slideshow. I know this is good enough. I barely slept after going home from the album wrap party and didn't even eat lunch. I just typed away on my computer, revised the sources, and made sure everything was perfect.

For this moment.

My entry to college and my get-out-of-jail-free card so I can be with Daniel.

"I got close to Daniel, and there was nothing—" I start.

Lloyd interrupts me, frowning. "Who the fuck is Daniel?"

"Rotten." I shake my head. *Rookie mistake.* "He just wasn't as interesting as we hoped. But he took me somewhere . . . *very* interesting." I slide the printed papers across his desk, feigning confidence. I tilt my chin up and use my grown-up journalist voice. "It's an exclusive club hidden in the residential area of LA. Rich and famous minors getting drunk and doing drugs openly. It's owned by some big guns in the entertainment industry, so there's a lot to be said here about exploitation." I make a dramatic pause. "I got many of them on video too. I have a flash drive."

Lloyd stares at me, like he's waiting for me to keep talking, but this is all I have. It's everything I got at the club during Mischief & Mayhem's album wrap party, when I told Rotten I needed a minute—to photograph and record video of all sorts of celebrities behaving badly.

And Lloyd is . . . unimpressed.

He sighs, rocking back and forth in his gamer chair. "There are tons of illegal bars in Los Angeles, Sasha. There aren't a ton of Rottens, though."

My throat goes dry and my heart sinks.

No, no, no.

He pushes the papers away, like he's allergic to them.

He won't even read it.

"That's not what we agreed on," he says.

To his credit, he sounds sincerely sorry.

My eyes burn, but I refuse to cry.

"There was no story on Rotten," I insist.

"Then there's no scholarship opportunity for you." He shrugs, leaning back. Washing his hands. Done with me. "I want to help you. I do. But I have to think of what will make us go viral. And an illegal club isn't it."

I shut my eyes and take a deep breath.

Daniel is a good guy. I can't ruin his career because of something I want.

I can't ruin what *I* have with *him.*

Standing up, I swallow the bitter taste in my mouth. "Thank you for the opportunity, then."

Lloyd gives me an empty smile. "If you change your mind before the end of the weekend, I'm still here."

Of course he is.

Vulture.

Mom's waiting for me with a bowl of popcorn in front of the TV when I get home from the LA Now office. I kick off my shoes by the doormat and leave my backpack by the door. She opens her arms, and I go to her, lose myself in her embrace until I'm not thinking about Lloyd or my failed article. Until the TV has captivated me. It's a documentary about wildlife. Mom loves those.

"When's your shift today at the superstore?" I ask.

"I start at five p.m. I can stay here with you a little longer." She pulls me closer, kisses the top of my head. I fall into her arms a little more. "Do you want to talk about whatever happened?"

"It's no use," I reply. "I've made up my mind."

And I hope it was the right choice. God, let that have been the right choice.

Mom nods, running her hands through my short hair. "Popcorn, then?"

We watch lions hunt deer while we eat popcorn and hug as if we're watching a soap opera. My heart still feels heavy, but not as much. I never told her I'd found a way to go to college on a scholarship, so she doesn't know I've lost it because I like a guy.

But I know she would understand.

Of all people, romantic Mom would understand.

I turn around so I'm facing Mom. She raises her eyebrows.

"Do you regret meeting him?" I ask.

She pauses. "Your father?"

I nod.

"Hmm." Mom chuckles. "I loved him very much. And he gave me the world's most wonderful gift: you. Of course I don't regret meeting him. If anything, I guess I love him to this day because he put you in my life."

Frowning, I shake my head. "Then imagine there's no me. No kid out of this relationship. Just the heartbreak, the lies. Do you still not regret it?"

Mom seems to take my question seriously. Her eyes dance around my face, like she's looking for whatever features are his. She traces my hooked nose with her finger, stopping at the tip.

"He was my first love. I don't regret it one bit."

"Even if he made you cry?" I press.

"Even if he made me cry," she insists.

The worst thing is that I believe her. And I wish I could believe that I'd feel the same. But right now I'm still scared that I've made the wrong decision.

SASHA:

how's the post-album high? lol

I scroll down my phone, trying to get past my last message, but there's nothing after it. He hasn't responded, even though I texted this afternoon, just a little before Mom left, and now it's almost nine p.m. My phone's never looked so annoying, and this is not how I wanted to spend my day off.

I feel restless, and I blame Lloyd for it. I don't want to be the kind of person who checks their phone nonstop for a reply from their crush when we're not even *official* yet—are we? But I can't focus on anything else. My thoughts keep going back to the phone and the unanswered text.

After a rushed dinner that consists of mac and cheese leftovers from lunch, I start obsessing.

We're supposed to be going on a date today. Santa Monica Pier, of all things. He was supposed to pick me up at eight, and now he's almost an hour late.

Yesterday at the club was magical, but the conversation with Lloyd has left me feeling a bit hollow. I know that seeing Daniel will fix everything, though.

If he just answers his phone.

I wish I could call Claire.

I go to the most obvious source—his Instagram page.

When I check his stories, there's a series of blinking lights, slurred words. A pretty tall brown girl dances at his side. She's big, with an arm around his shoulders, wearing a leather V-cut dress. The front of his shirt's drenched in sweat, as if he's been dancing a lot. His eyes are bloodshot and distant, and he sips on a red drink before yelling at Sam to stop recording. His location is tagged—they're at the same club we went to yesterday. The one I tried to pitch the story about.

He ghosted me all day, but now he's partying with his friends? We went out *yesterday,* and it was so . . . magical.

I hold my breath.

Something doesn't feel right.

I know—God, I *know*—that things are wrong. I felt it in my gut the second he didn't reply to my text. He has never gone this long without texting me before.

Daniel is drunk af.

And I am . . . a colossal idiot.

His words ring in my ears: *Never even had any alcohol. First kiss. Special.*

I drop the phone back onto the table, my hands trembling.

It's all there, the evidence that he lied to me, and for a good journalist, that should be more than enough to turn away and never look back. But the awful thing is that I care about him. I really *like* him. And clearly I managed to fall into the exact same trap that all these other girls have probably fallen into as well. What a cruel thing to lie about, that there were no other girls at all.

My nostrils flare in frustration, my eyes burning, but I swallow it all down. I will not cry yet. I need to believe that there's more to the story.

Please. Let there be more.

I leave and get an Uber, which is crazy-expensive, but at least I remember the location of the club. The driver isn't the most pleasant guy, throwing random comments about my *killer* outfit. It's not only that it's inappropriate and he's way too old, but also that I'm not trying to look pretty. I may be wearing makeup and a tight dress so I don't stand out in the club, but I feel like I'm dressed in armor.

The security people let me in once I say the password, the same silly line from yesterday. I'm not sure what I would have done if that hadn't worked out. All I know is that I have tunnel vision. I don't care about anything else. The biggest story of the year could break right in front of me, and I would completely miss it.

I go straight to the VIP area, but the band isn't sitting where they were yesterday. My heart is already thumping out of control. But I do find them.

Eventually I find him.

Daniel looks the same as he did in his Instagram story. He's sitting on the VIP couch with the same girl from before, and they're sharing the red drink. Daniel says something into her ear, and she laughs.

I don't hate her. I truly don't. But I want to push her away and tell her that, whatever he's saying, he's lying to her.

My eyes burn way too much now. I tell myself it's the dry ice smoke that's spilling out onto the club's dance floor.

My legs don't want to take me there, but they've taken me this far.

I force one foot in front of the other. Security doesn't want to let me into the VIP area this time. They're full-on blocking me, so I scream his name. When he doesn't respond, I try again, shouting, "Rotten!" and it feels so thoroughly humiliating.

But he listens this time.

He raises his eyebrows, gives me an aloof smile, and tells security to let me in.

I step onto the elevated stage with a sense of otherness that makes me feel like throwing up.

With each step I take toward him, I wish I weren't here.

My eyes are glued on this guy who's slumped on the couch with a girl on his arm, so drunk that he can barely keep his eyes open. Just yesterday I made a decision for him that cost me my future. And now here he is. Now here we are.

"Sasha, hi," he says, but the words sound like all one syllable somehow.

"Daniel . . ." I hold my breath. "What are you doing?"

"I . . . ," he starts, then pauses, giggling and shrugging. "You know what? I don't know," he slurs. *Iroknow.* "This is my friend. . . . What's your name again? Did you tell me your name?"

"Amanda!" She laughs, like it's not the first time he's asked her tonight.

I'm going to be sick. I'm going to be sick, I'm going to be sick, I'm going to be sick.

Amanda looks between us, like she's confused.

"Get lost, Amanda," I say, eyes firmly on him.

That's enough for her. She sighs, either annoyed or

amused, or perhaps a little bit of both. She gathers her purse, a small silver thing with a lot of sequins, and passes me without a word. No catty remarks, at least. I couldn't deal with that. I can barely deal with what's in front of me.

I can't even move any closer.

My fists are balled, and I'm doing all I can to not cry.

"Why did you talk to her like that? She was nice," Daniel says.

I shake my head. "Oh my God, Daniel. How much did you drink?"

"Lil' bit. Lil' lots." He shrugs again.

"I'm such an idiot . . . ," I murmur. And then my resolve hardens. I deserve some closure. "You lied. You lied about everything. You're an asshole, Rotten."

Huh. I thought that'd feel better. Instead I feel closer to tears.

"Why are you . . . Why did you call me an asshole?" he asks. Suddenly he sounds broken too. He sounds like his heart is breaking into a thousand pieces, like he's standing at the edge of a cliff. "Why aren't you calling me *Daniel* anymore?"

That's what does it for me. The way he sounds so *sincere* in his heartbreak, like our relationship or whatever it was meant so much to him, when he was so clearly lying about everything. God, I could punch his handsome kissable face.

I frown, taking a step back. My voice grows louder.

"Do you get off on playing with girls' feelings? Is that what this is? All that talk about how I was your first kiss . . . I should've known. I really can't believe I fell for that."

He gets up. I think he's going to try to stop me from leaving. He says, "You fell for me?"

Choked up, I answer, "I fell for your *lies*."

I don't think he really listens to what I say. He's still processing something else, studying me closely. It's weird how somber he sounds next, for a drunk guy.

"I think I figured you out . . . your big mystery," he says. I freeze. "You always believe the worst in people. Maybe you're even addicted to it."

And then he sits down again and grabs his stupid red drink.

"Wow, just . . . Shut up, Rotten." I sigh, tired. I can't hold the tears in for much longer. *I want to go home.* "I don't want to hear from you again."

I turn to leave, but when I reach the end of their VIP booth, I run into Sam and Wade. And of course they don't let me go. They're like a wall of tall teen energy blocking my exit from this nightmare.

"Sasha? I didn't know you were coming," Wade says, smiling brightly. He's wearing a fake nose ring. Or maybe it's real and new. I don't care.

"I'm leaving, actually." I try to walk around them, but they're both big and don't seem to get the memo.

Wade says, "Did Rotten fall asleep? Wait, I want to

introduce you to—where's Amanda? She was here. Did you see her?"

Great. Everyone knows Amanda already.

"Like I said, I'm leaving." I offer them my best fake smile.

"Was Rotten a dick to you?" Sam asks. "He's just wasted. Don't listen to him. He's totally into you. I think the bet was just an excuse to get closer to you."

This stops me dead in my tracks.

I move closer to Sam, frowning at him, my heart racing. "The *bet*?"

Sam nods. "Yeah, like . . . the bet we had earlier in the summer, when we were arguing about album tracks." He turns to Wade, who's not entirely registering the conversation. "Right? What did we say? That he had to date a girl for the *whole* summer, or just most of the summer?"

Wade blinks slowly at him. "Uh, I think we just said summer. But we already agreed he won last night."

I squeeze my eyes shut, like it will all just go away.

Of course.

I was a bet, and he is a liar.

I never should've considered giving up a dream scholarship for him. UCLA should've come first. I never should've believed, even for one second, that I could be any more than what I am. Just a little girl in this sea of arrogant, self-entitled celebrities. It hurts now, but I'm going to make it hurt more for him.

My eyes are blurry with tears.

I don't listen to Sam's or Wade's words as I force my way out of the crowd.

I was a girl on a mission, but now my mission has changed.

The truth shall set you free, right? I hope that's real.

Because I'm about to hit Rotten with loads of truth.

23

Daniel

I've had headaches before. This is so much different—and so much worse.

I groan and curl into a ball, hugging one of my pillows while pulling the light blanket around me. My whole body hurts, but my head really throbs with pain. I feel like there's a little man inside my skull with a massive hammer.

I can *hear* the pain.

Is this what a hangover feels like? I try to open my eyes, but the light that comes through the drawn curtains, although dim, assaults my vision in a way that's nearly obscene. I pull the blanket over my head, vowing to never leave this protective fort again.

As I lie here, it all starts coming back to me. I remember Helena yelling at me when I got home from the club. Calling me names in Portuguese, saying that I shouldn't have run off last night, that she'd been worried.

I remember puking on her shoes.

Oh God. I puked on my sister's shoes. She's going to murder me.

I'm not 100 percent sure how I got home. I think it might have been Wade or Sam who drove me, or was it Sam's cousin? I think her name was Audrey or Andressa. Something vaguely Brazilian? *Amanda.*

I remember getting drinks from the bar. Something red. Something kind of disgusting. It burned my throat and numbed my tongue. After a while, it didn't even feel like it was liquid anymore.

The thought of it makes my stomach turn. My hands cover my middle protectively. I seriously don't know how people do this. Have I partied wrong somehow? I expected the numbness. Welcomed it, even. But something must've gone wrong. I can't accept that everyone ingests this type of disgusting—actually, I need to stop thinking about that shit I drank or I might puke again.

I think Amanda came to the club with Wade. Were they flirting? I was crying at some point, couldn't stop sniffing and trying to look tough, and I think she noticed and was nice about it. She was really nice. I need to thank her. And then she disappeared, and I was alone again.

Get lost, Amanda.

The words echo in my mind, and I sit up abruptly, way too fast for someone with a hangover. I almost have to lie down again, but I regain my balance—*Sasha.* Sasha was there. For some reason, she showed up.

"And we had a fight," I say out loud.

My voice sounds off, my throat too dry. I wipe the sleep off my eyes with the backs of my hands, and groggily make my way to the en suite bathroom, going over our fight in my head.

I should call her. Yes, I have to call her. She shouldn't have been there.

I shouldn't have been there.

I stare at the bathroom. I'm a mess.

The bathroom is like a murder scene. My clothes from yesterday are on the floor, the wet towel too, and the shower is still dripping ominously. There's evidence that I vomited up the red drink all over the bathroom tiles.

Even though it feels like I'm a little closer to actual hell with every step, I take another shower. To try to relax my sore muscles, wash the sweat out of my hair, the sleep off my face, and try to put my thoughts in order.

Yesterday keeps coming back to me, and I hate it all.

Mom's heart attack, Helena crying, Mom stabilizing but me not being able to see her because the hospital signal isn't good. Something as ridiculous as bad Wi-Fi standing between me and one of the people I love most in the world.

I didn't think I'd see Sasha at the club. I didn't *want* to see anyone who truly cared. I wanted to disappear for a night.

Instead I just hurt everyone more.

Once I'm out of the shower, I make a list in my head of the people I have to apologize to. Dad, for one, but mostly Helena and Sasha. But when I leave the bathroom, a towel wrapped around my waist, my sister's sitting on the bed with wide eyes, staring down at her phone.

My heart stops.

"Is Mom—?" I ask.

She looks up at me, still wearing an expression of shock. She shakes her head. "No, she's fine. She'll go home sometime today, actually. I talked with Dad earlier, while you were still asleep."

Relief shoots through me, and I allow myself to smile.

But she's still looking at me like that, so I add, "Listen, I know I was a dick to you yesterday, and I don't plan on getting away with it. I'll make—"

Helena looks down at the phone again, and that's when I realize that it isn't hers. It's *my* phone she's holding. "We'll talk about yesterday later." She gets up, still holding my phone in both hands. "Get dressed. I'm waiting for you downstairs with an aspirin. We have to talk."

As promised, my sister has an aspirin and a glass of water ready. I take them and wordlessly sit across from her in the kitchen. She's still holding my phone, and I'm still feeling choked up. If this isn't about our mom or the fact that I puked all over Helena's shoes yesterday, I have no clue what it could possibly be about.

"I'm sorry," I say. "Desculpa, mana."

She gestures dismissively. "Later, Daniel." I can tell that

she's still annoyed with me, but this is more serious. She puts my phone on the table facedown and takes a deep breath before looking at me. "How are you feeling?"

"Like shit." I shrug. "My head hurts a lot. Feels like my body was run over by a truck. I want to go back to bed."

"That's called a hangover," she comments, matter-of-factly, and then her expression changes. Almost businesslike, she adds, "You can't go back to bed. You have a meeting soon with your agent."

"What? No, I—"

She cuts me off, putting a hand up so I'll stop talking. I do.

"She called." Helena sits up a little straighter. "She thought it was better if . . . I talk to you before her. But she still needs to see you today."

My mind races. Looking past Helena, I see the clock on the wall, and my eyebrows shoot up.

"Wait, it's almost two? How is it almost two? Did I sleep— How did— Why did you let me sleep so much?"

Helena rolls her eyes. "Sorry. I thought you looked trashed and let you sleep in."

"No, I mean—" I stop myself. "I just never sleep that much." I'm nervous and my hands are jittery. In the absence of some yarn and a needle, I ball them into fists. It doesn't work to contain my anxiety, so I cross my arms over my chest. Clearing my throat, I ignore the pounding in my head. "What does Bobbi want you to tell me? What do you need to talk to me about?"

Helena looks like a mirror in a fun house. My sister, but somehow different. I can see enough of myself in her features that it unnerves me all the more to see how much she struggles to speak. How she won't look me in the eye.

"Someone . . ." She closes her eyes, takes another deep breath, then opens them again, as if forcing herself to face me. "No, not someone. Sasha."

"What about Sasha?" I frown.

Helena gives me a curt nod. "Did you know she works for a magazine, Daniel?"

It doesn't sound accusatory. It doesn't sound like curiosity either.

It sounds like she's afraid I might say yes. It sounds like she's afraid, period.

"She works in a diner," I say, correcting her. "It's her summer job." Helena gives me a pitying look. I grit my teeth. "I've seen her work there, Helena. She works *there*."

Helena's shoulders sag. "She may work there too, but that doesn't mean she isn't a reporter, Dani." She touches my phone tentatively. "Do you want to see her byline? Click her bio to see the picture?"

I don't understand what she means.

But my heart still sinks.

She reaches for my hand. "She—She wrote a piece about you for an online magazine. There are audio clips of your conversations, and some text message screenshots." Helena presses her lips. I see that this hurts her too. "There's even a selfie of you with your crochet kit, Dani."

I try to swallow the knot in my throat. "We were—we were showing each other what we were doing. She was reading a biography, and I was crocheting."

She shakes her head. "I recommend that you don't go online for a bit. It's all over social media. Everyone's ridiculing you." In the same breath, she reaches for my hand again, and this time doesn't let me yank it away. "Look, I don't think there's *anything* wrong about *anything* that you are. You are my little brother, and you are *perfect.* But people don't understand. They have this stereotype in their head, of what a rock star should be. And you're not it."

"Oh my God." I pause. "Que bosta," I swear.

And then more colorful swear words come.

Helena doesn't say anything, just watches me closely.

Sasha was a reporter.

Sasha used me.

Sasha, who was my first kiss, is also a reporter, and wrote an exposé on me.

Suddenly my headache doesn't feel like such a big deal anymore.

"Can you take me to Bobbi?"

"Sure. You shouldn't drive like this." She gives my hand a little squeeze. "Let me get my wallet."

Before she lets go of my hand, I ask her, "If they kick me out of the band, and we have to move back to Brazil . . . will it be okay?"

"Eventually, yeah." She comes closer and plants a kiss

on the top of my head. "But if that happens, you're going to buy Otis a plane ticket to Brazil every summer. Okay?"

It's the first smile I've seen from her today. I nod, trying to smile back, even though I still feel dumbstruck. "Okay, yeah. Deal."

I'm standing in front of the door to Bobbi's office, like I'm carrying the bomb that will land on everyone inside that room and destroy everything. Like it's my fault, even though I know it's Sasha's . . . But isn't it mine too? Isn't it my fault for trusting her?

My hand pauses on the doorknob. It's so cold.

Eventually I turn the doorknob and make my way into the room where the rest of my bandmates are sitting. I can tell they were talking, because they all get very quiet, Sam and Wade both avoiding my eyes. Penny gets up from her leather chair and meets me halfway across the room. "Rotten." She takes a deep breath. "How, um, how are you?"

I'm at a loss for words.

How *am* I?

I shrug, and try to give her a small smile. It's not super convincing.

She puts a hand on my shoulder and guides me to the conference table. It's too big for only the four of us, but we sit toward the end of the table, so Wade and Sam are facing

Penny and me. I'm staring down at the wooden table, trying to ease my breathing.

They all try to talk at the same time.

Wade says, "Have you—?"

Sam says, "We need to ta—"

Penny says, "It's on Twitt—"

I look up at them. "I am so sorry. I messed this up." I slump in my seat, running a hand over my head. "I'm so sorry for everything. On the way here, my sister told me there are pictures and videos of you all too. I shouldn't have exposed you to this. I shouldn't have—"

Wade interrupts me. "Have you read it?"

Shaking my head, I look away again. "I haven't had the courage to. Helena said it's probably better if I don't. She's afraid it'll hurt me or something, like that's avoidable."

"It's not," Penny argues. "Read it."

She takes her phone, a model like mine but with a golden case, and thumbs away at the screen. Then she's passing it to me, the article penned by Sasha on the LA Now website open in her web browser. Just seeing Sasha's name under the headline FAKE BAD BOY SECRETLY BAD AT LOVE makes my skin itch. Sure, she knows I'm a fake. Sure, she knows I'm a fraud. But isn't she one too?

It's a long piece, and I'm absorbing only half of it. She writes about how we first met by accident, and how ambivalent I was. Part real and part not. Part Rotten and part Daniel. Not entirely one or the other. A mix of both. A lie and a truth untold.

She calls me out for lying, for showing up drunk at the club yesterday. She writes that it's easier for me to let the lies define who I am instead of fighting for myself. A few lines jump out at me:

Daniel-slash-Rotten made a bet with his friends that our relationship would last through the summer. They got into a pitiful argument about creative differences. This is all I ever was to him: a way to settle the deal.

He's not a bad boy. But he's still an asshole.

She knows about the bet.

I don't want to keep reading anymore.

I quickly look up at my bandmates. Penny is the only one who's watching me, waiting for me to be done with the piece. I look down again, reading that last sentence over and over again. It doesn't even surprise me that she knows about the bet. She is a journalist after all.

Trying to swallow the bitter taste in my throat, I keep reading, trying to make sense of the next words.

. . . I hate him for it. I hate him for it all.

The worst part isn't that he lied to everyone, that he let others assume whatever they wanted instead of speaking up for himself. It's not about the bet. It's not even about the fact that I was ready to give up on my dreams for him.

What I hate the most about Daniel is that he is *Rotten. Not because he's a cool bad boy but because he doesn't care. I hate him for making me fall in love with him, and then breaking my heart.*

This is where the piece ends.

Her final words burn in my mind as I put the phone

down. Penny carefully takes her phone back and exhales. "I'm sorry," she says.

I didn't mean to. Break Sasha's heart.

I fell for her too.

Straightening up in my chair, I try to push back the confused feelings in my head and heart.

"I should have been up-front with you all from the beginning," I say, looking intently at them until each looks back. "She's right about something. . . . I didn't have the nerve to show my true self. Not even to my band."

Wade tries, "It's cool—"

But it's not.

Penny offers, "You should have. We would've stood by you from the start."

I don't know if that's true, but the way she squeezes my hand on top of the table right now makes me feel like it is. I nod slowly. "I just felt like I didn't belong. Like I wasn't adding anything to Mischief and Mayhem."

Wade chuckles. "What's more mischievous than creating a hell of a lot of mayhem right around the time our album debuts?"

I know he's joking, but I still feel horrible about it. I'm ready to apologize again, when Sam speaks up. "What do you mean, Rotten?" He's frowning. "You just said you felt like you didn't belong."

"Can you all just call me Daniel now?" I ask, a murmur instead of a question.

But Sam is impatient. "Okay, then, Daniel. What do you mean by that?"

I run my hands over my head, feeling the shaved sides with my palms as I try to put my thoughts in order enough to speak. "It's just . . . you all had this thing going already when I came here. And I'm not as good as the rest of you. I can't even . . ." I take a deep breath, gaining confidence. "I can't even speak up when it really matters."

"You're such a baby," Sam deadpans. Wade slaps his arm, giving him horrified eyes, and Sam sighs. "I'm sorry. I shouldn't have said that. But *obviously* you belong in the band. We wouldn't even have made it past the first rounds of *Making Music!* without you." His expression softens slightly. "I know we haven't always made the space for you to make your voice heard, and that's on us. But we're going to do better. We're a *band*. All of us."

I'm speechless. I kind of want to reach for Sam across this table and hug him.

"So I'm not . . . kicked out of the band yet?" I try.

"Not so fast." Wade raises a finger. "I mean, nobody's kicking you out. But there's something else." He shoots Sam a look. "Right?"

I turn to Penny, but she shrugs. "This is new to me too. Tweedledee and Tweedledum have their own secrets."

Sam takes such a dramatic deep breath that it feels like he's going to suck all the air out of the room. Wade gives him a little encouraging push, and Sam speaks. "It was me. I can't tell you how sorry I am . . . but it was my fault."

"You . . . what? Ghostwrote this entire piece and just let Sasha take the credit?" I ask.

Not sure why I'm trying to be funny. I'm nervous.

Sam doesn't smile. He only shakes his head. "I told her about the bet." Before I can react, Penny yells his name, and he adds, more to her than me, "I was *beyond* drunk, and I didn't mean to! I wasn't trying to sabotage Daniel."

I nod. "Thanks. For telling me the truth and for apologizing."

Sam still looks like he's holding his breath. "Do you—?"

I offer him a half smile. "Yeah, I accept your apology. But Penny's not wrong. Next time, talking would be a, um, better option. Easier, at least."

Penny side-eyes me. "I mean, *you're* one to talk, Mr. Communicative."

My smile widens, and she chuckles.

It's not okay, and I'm not all right. None of us are. But maybe it's going to be fine.

24

Sasha

The board—aka Lloyd and his parents—doesn't take long to announce the scholarship.

I got it.

Lloyd pays me for the story too, a whopping two hundred bucks, more than I made with any photograph I took before, and he guarantees it's the competitive rate. Some Googling tells me that he's not lying *entirely*, even though I know that I had a major scoop and maybe should have held out for more. But it's okay. I wasn't even counting on the money for my first byline.

Mom doesn't know the full story, but she knows enough to invite over two friends and three aunts, who I'm not sure are distant cousins or related to us at all, to celebrate with two big bottles of champagne. This is the biggest accomplishment our family has ever had: I've got a huge college scholarship.

Mom pops the champagne and then pours it into everyone's glasses. Everyone oohs and aahs, and then Mom calls everyone's attention, clearing her throat and getting up onto one of the chairs. "Hey. I want to say something."

Everyone looks at her, but I look down at my plastic glass of champagne. Her friend Ximena bought those, fancy and painted in silver. It's actually very sweet.

"Sasha has always loved music, even when she was still in my belly." She smiles, placing her hands protectively over her stomach. "I would play her the classics, from Janis to Cazuza, and she'd kick around like she was having a party!" On cue, everyone laughs. Our small living room is so crowded. "When she learned to write, she told me she wanted to write about music. And I believed her. I swear to God, I did. Because there's nothing my little girl can't do."

Mom pauses, getting emotional. Her eyes are shiny with tears, but we all know that she's not going to let herself cry. She raises her glass, and everyone raises their glass along with her, even me, from the back of the room.

"To my baby, who impressed her bosses so much with her work that she won the very first LA Now Group of Thinkers Scholarship for Upcoming Voices in Journalism!"

Everyone cheers and drinks.

I stare at them all, each downing their plastic cup of champagne. One of Mom's coworkers yells a congrats in Spanish, and soon everyone is gathering around Mom for second servings of champagne. Someone pops open the second bottle.

I should be celebrating with them.

But I'm empty.

I don't deserve this celebration. I don't deserve Mom's

tears, just like I didn't really deserve Lloyd himself nearly crying with happiness that he'd published such a scoop, or Vanessa winking at me and telling me that I'd made it onto the team.

An hour later, the people at our house have multiplied. More friends of Mom's, of course. They have brought beer and wine, and everyone's having a great time, so I don't want to upset anyone. I'm sitting outside, glued to my phone, scrolling down a BuzzFeed article called "10 Times Rotten Slipped but We Didn't Want to Believe" when Mom surprises me by sitting down next to me.

With her huge grin and her bouncy side ponytail, she looks even younger than she is. She gives me a wink, and I wink back at her, putting my phone down.

"Why didn't you invite any of your friends?" she asks. "It's basically a middle-aged party in here."

"None of your friends are that old," I say, correcting her, but she shrugs. I can't tell her that I basically have no friends, especially now. So I shrug back.

"How about Claire?" she presses. "I haven't seen her in a few days. Why isn't she here?"

"I haven't seen her either."

That's not the whole truth. I asked my boss to change my shifts so I wouldn't be paired with Claire at the diner.

"But have you told her the news? She'll be so thrilled for you."

"She's probably heard about it," I murmur.

Mom watches me carefully.

"Is something going on? You should be so much happier. I thought . . . I thought this is what you always wanted."

It's so hard to put into words what you feel when you're not exactly sure what that is. How do I tell her that I'm ashamed but I'm not even sure if I *should* be? Maybe I've done the right thing. Maybe he deserves it. He hasn't called or confronted me about it, so he must know that he had it coming.

Bringing my knees closer to my chest, I just groan.

Mom puts a hand on my back. "Give me a word. Only one word."

That's easy. I blurt out, without thinking: "Scared."

She reaches over my shoulders so she's hugging me. "I've heard college can be scary. But if anyone can do it, it's you."

I nod, pretending that's all it is.

She leaves me alone, and I stare off into the distance, thinking back to his car parked in front of my house. It's not long before my finger hovers over his name in my contact list. Should I? Do I even have the right? Whether he deserved it or not, I'm not sure I should call him now.

But I'm alone again, and the party's still going on, and I miss him.

I miss his gap-toothed smile, his gorgeous brown eyes, his funny stories. I even miss his kiss.

Perhaps I'm the most delusional person in the world for missing him.

But whatever.

I'm still human.

I press call.

25

Daniel

My blood goes cold when I see Sasha's name on my phone screen.

Helena turns to me and asks, "Do you need to take that?"

I shake my head and put the phone on silent mode.

Sitting up straight again, I look back at Helena's phone, which is positioned in the middle of the kitchen table. "Sorry for the interruption. You were saying, Dad?"

On the small screen, Dad looks like he's aged twenty years in the last week alone. He's got bags under his eyes. It can't have been something recent, but I'm only noticing it now—how his hair is thinning, how fragile he looks. It makes me feel queasy.

"Yeah." He's wandering around the house, apparently in circles. Helena has asked him to stop already, but he seems too anxious. He doesn't have crocheting for crises like this. "So, Mom is okay. Your aunt Giseli wants to stay over for a few days at least to help with things, even though your mother says that's not necessary. But I'm glad. I'm—"

"Mom's home," Helena breathes out, looking at me.

I nod, feeling my heart race. "Can we see her?" I ask. "Please." Helena puts a hand on my shoulder and gives it a little squeeze. I want to tell my sister I love her, but she'll call me a baby if I do that.

On the little screen, we see Dad enter their bedroom. Mom takes the phone from him. She holds it with a frown until she can focus on us, sitting close together so we'll both appear on the screen. Then she cracks a smile.

"Look at the two of you. My best creations."

Somehow she looks exactly the same.

I don't care about the news and the tabloids. I only care that everything is going to be okay. That things are already well on their way to being okay.

Even if Sasha's still calling me.

I swallow that bitter feeling and turn my attention back to my mother. "Mom. I'm so happy to see you."

Although we own a dishwasher here, no Brazilian household would be caught actually *using* one, so we still handwash all our dishes. After our late-night snack, Helena's washing the dishes and I'm drying them, and we're in much better spirits. Talking to Mom helped. So I'm not expecting it when she says, "It was Sasha calling you, right?"

I freeze.

Helena sighs. "How do you feel?"

"Tired. It's almost three in the morning and I can't sleep." I chuckle dryly, and she glares at me. I make a face, grabbing a plate to dry. "Betrayed. That's about it."

"Still in love?" she presses.

Why does my sister ask things she already knows the answer to?

I give her a long look.

"It will pass," I say.

For a long moment, the only thing we hear is the running water in the sink. Then my sister makes an annoyed sound, her tongue clicking the roof of her mouth three times. *Tsk, tsk, tsk.*

"What is it?" I ask.

"Your phone. She's calling again. If you don't pick up, she's going to keep calling."

I pause, looking at her . . .

"Go," she says.

So I do. Feeling like I'm moving through sand with each step, I get my phone from the kitchen table and go to the living room. Sasha's name is on the screen.

I answer the call.

Neither of us says a word for a second.

"Daniel?" she tries, eventually.

I take a deep breath.

"Yeah," I say.

Again we're quiet.

My heart feels like it's beating at the speed of light. I am so anxious that I feel like I might undo the hem of my shirt if I keep messing with it. I walk straight to the armchair, but it still takes me a moment to sit and pull my legs up.

She doesn't say a word.

"Are you still there?" I say.

"I'm trying to figure out what to say to you." She sounds like she's been crying, and I feel like a jerk, even though . . . even though I shouldn't. Because she's the one who ruined everything. She's the one who wrote an *exposé* on me! But I still hate that she sounds like this. "Are you angry at me?" she asks.

I consider it.

Believe it or not, I don't know if I've ever been. Hurt? Yes. One hundred percent. Angry, though? I don't know. But if she expects me to just forgive her and move on somehow . . . well, I'm not sure I can.

I don't even know if that's what she wants.

"I miss you," she adds, before I can answer her question.

And I miss her too. So much. But that wouldn't be right to say either.

I know because it doesn't feel right to hear it.

"Was this your plan from the get-go?" I finally ask.

Do I even want to know? It won't make a difference. It's only going to hurt more, but—

"Yes," she admits, and now I'm sure she's crying. My stomach sinks, and I want to cry too, but I'm too shocked to do anything. I didn't really expect her to say *yes*. "But then things changed. I wasn't going to do it anymore. I tried not to. I promise I tried not to do it."

"Wow, okay, you accidentally wrote a viral takedown of my character."

My throat is dry. My voice is half-gone. I'm glad this won't take long. I'm glad my sister will be here soon, with her reluctant hugs and I-told-you-sos. I don't want to be alone.

"No, it wasn't an accident, but—you lied to me," she says, her voice stronger now. "You said you'd never been drunk, and then you stood me up for our date. And, well, you were at that club and you were completely wasted—"

"What?" I nearly bark. "Sasha, my mom just had a heart attack. I thought she was going to die. I was sad and lonely and wanted to feel numb. That was the first time I ever had a drink in my life." I pause, then add, as an afterthought, "Do you want me to repeat that? This time you can record it."

"Wait, what? What happened?" she asks. I don't respond. Her initial confusion settles, and I hear her sharp inhale of breath. "I . . . I didn't know. Why didn't you talk to me?"

"Because I didn't want to show you a bad part of me. But I guess now the whole world knows every part of me." I chuckle.

"But what about the bet?" she presses. "I felt so *used,* Daniel. Everything felt like a lie."

And I know she has the right to be pissed about it, but the way she uses it as an excuse just makes me more upset.

"Yeah, there was a stupid bet, and I'm sorry for that. I would've told you, but the bet became so pointless to me so fast. I didn't lie about anything else."

She gets very quiet on the other end.

So quiet that the silence between us expands and I feel like I might drown. Before I get lost in it, I tell her, "Please don't call me again."

With that, I hang up.

26

Sasha

It's half a week later when our manager Raj decides that he doesn't care about my attempts to run away from Claire and puts us together on the same shift, her at the checkout, me waiting tables. It's awkward at best.

The truth is that I really, really want to talk to her.

I miss Claire. I miss my best friend.

And I miss *him* too.

I smile at the newcomers who sit in my section, and ask, "What can I get you today?"

The shift goes by like this, customer after customer filling the booths, while I avoid eye contact with Claire. I think I might miraculously get away with it, but then it's break time, and since it's the tail end of the summer, there's only one thing to do: steal an ice cream cone and take it to the back. When I push my way out the back door, Claire's already sitting on an overturned can next to the dumpster, with a cone of her own.

Time stretches in the few seconds that follow.

She says, "I'd say hi, but you might run if I do."

"You don't get to be passive-aggressive." I walk forward slowly until I'm sitting on the curb, two feet away from her. "You're the one in the wrong here, you know."

"I know." She breathes out heavily. "But you've been avoiding me like the plague. What am I supposed to think? It still hurts that you wouldn't take my calls or let me *try* to make things right."

I unwrap my cone and take a bite of the ice cream.

"Are things still bad?" she asks, her voice small.

After I locked down all my profiles, things actually got better. I still get tagged in a lot of stuff, but I disabled the notifications so I won't see it. It's exhausting. Mom keeps giving me hints that we can talk about it if I want to; she finally seems to have connected the dots between the attacks online, the scholarship, and the article I wrote that went viral. But she won't say anything to me directly. She's waiting for me to be ready.

I don't know if there's any way I could be ready to talk about all of this. I feel so embarrassed half the time. The other half I just feel defeated.

This is not how getting everything you've ever dreamed of is supposed to feel.

"They are, but not for the same reasons," I say.

Claire risks a look at me over her shoulder. "I read your article. It's, um, well written."

That actually makes me laugh.

"Thanks."

This time when we're quiet, it's not as bad anymore. It's not awkward, just a little uncomfortable. It doesn't make me want to fill the silence. It doesn't make me feel like I should run and never look back.

"You could've told me about the arti—" she starts.

"I couldn't have," I say. "You would've tried to stop me."

"You're right, I would have," Claire admits. She turns to me and studies my face. "I really am sorry about what I did. I basically threw you under the bus. I wasn't thinking. But I know that's not a good enough excuse." Another pause, and our eyes meet for real now. "I really miss you."

I try swallowing the knot in my throat. It doesn't quite go away.

"I know you didn't mean to. I think I just needed some time. . . . I miss you too."

I add the last part really fast, *Imissyoutoo*, but she hears it just fine. I feel a little lighter. And I feel like crying at the same time, because I don't feel so alone with her by my side.

"Do you forgive me?" she asks.

There's so much expectation in her eyes, like she might collapse if I say no.

It makes me smile.

"I do. Thanks for apologizing."

"OhmyGodthankGodI'vebeensomiserable." She says it all in one breath.

We laugh, and she comes to sit beside me on the curb. Joined at the hip again, our bodies close even though it's so hot. I feel a sense of contentment that I haven't felt in days, and reward myself by taking another bite of my ice cream.

"You don't have to tell me if you don't want to," Claire starts, and I know exactly what this is about, even if she takes her time with the words. "Or if you're not ready, that's fine too. But you don't seem very happy, so I'm just wondering. Are you? Happy?"

"No," I answer, a bit too fast, a bit too sincerely. "I miss him. And he doesn't want to talk to me anymore. I made this big mistake, but—but I don't know if I can even be entirely sorry. I'm sorry I hurt him. I'm sorry about *how* I did things. But I'm going to be able to go to college now, Claire. I couldn't say no to that. I—I just should've been honest with him."

"We have ten minutes before Raj comes for us. Start talking."

This time I don't leave any details out. I tell her everything, from our first accidental encounter, to him bringing my jacket back here to Angeles Diner. I tell her about Lloyd, how dirty I felt right after he proposed the story. I tell her about my struggle with money and wanting to go to college. Claire listens to me as I tell her how I fooled myself into justifying the article. How every time we were together, I kept fighting my feelings for Daniel.

I tell her about the album wrap party, about me deciding to write a story about the club and how that wasn't enough for Lloyd. Daniel taking me to the rooftop, kissing me under the LA stars. I confess my phone call to him and how he asked me to stop calling.

How I've tried to stop thinking about him as well.

When I'm done, she's holding my hand. I didn't realize she'd reached for it.

"I want to make things right," I tell her. "I wish I could tell him how I really feel."

Claire considers this. She gives me a hard look, but a smile plays at the corner of her mouth. "If only you knew a massive M and M fan who knew their band schedule better than they know it themselves. . . ."

I hold my breath, a question in my eyes.

She answers that unspoken question with a grin.

27

Daniel

It's Mischief & Mayhem's first time on *The Late Late Show,* and it's different from anything else we've done. We *have* to make this work, so that everyone talks about how great our new album is instead of what a fraud I am.

I'm jittery and nervous, but the light atmosphere makes it better. Sam and Wade have been cracking joke after joke even though that probably just means they're nervous too. Penny is quieter, and on the car ride here, she told me she thinks tonight's performance will be our most important yet. I feel the same. There's this big question mark in the air, like if we perform well enough, then maybe we're good enough to really make it in the music industry. If we don't, we're just another failed reality-show project.

We still have a half hour in the green room before being called. It's the biggest green room I've ever been in, much bigger than the one we had at *Making Music!* There are three black leather couches, and one of the walls is entirely covered with a mirror. Our agent, Bobbi, is here, sitting across from us, looking chic in an all-white suit (which she says is not white, it's *ice*). She's mostly been trying to keep our spirits up, even though we're nervous and overwhelmed by the pressure to make tonight's show epic.

The last few days, we've rehearsed almost nonstop, and I am confident we won't completely ruin it. Penny is our spokesperson for the interview portion of our appearance—so if the host asks about Sasha's piece, Penny can deflect. Wade is great at cracking jokes at the right moment to lighten the mood, and Sam can charm the pants off pretty much anyone, so all I have to concentrate on is playing my guitar. Hopefully I can manage not to screw it up.

I get my phone out, go to my messages, and start typing something to Sasha before I even think about it. Then I stop myself, because *what am I doing*? We're not speaking. We don't do this anymore.

The band still has some time before we perform. I'm anxious, and with no needle or yarn.

"Don't do it," Sam says, by my side.

Bobbi looks up from her phone, frowns briefly at us, and looks down again.

"Don't Google yourself. It's what you're thinking about, isn't it?" he presses.

It wasn't, but I nod, exchanging a smile with him.

Bobbi takes a very deep breath, and asks, "Is the article still bothering you, Daniel?"

The press still calls me *Rotten,* but it feels good that none of the people around me call me *Rotten* anymore. It's like I've had a second chance, like I'm being reintroduced.

"Yeah. I just . . . I know how much we all worked for this, and now that the album's released, everyone should be talking about our music. Instead everyone's just gossiping about me."

Penny gives Bobbi a long look. "Is it as bad as he says?"

Bobbi sighs heavily, putting her phone down in her lap. "There is a lot of chatter about you and your private life, but that's nothing new. I won't lie and say that every outlet is taking you guys seriously, because I'd be lying. But I will say that the general public is even more in love with you than ever."

Wade makes a funny face. "They're seeing you through Sasha's eyes. You know she still has feelings for you, right, bro?"

Sam slouches on the couch. "I mean, obviously." He blows out a breath. "Listen, if I knew I could get an even bigger fan base by being a fake bad boy, I would have done it months ago."

Penny pets his head amicably. "You couldn't have pulled it off. You can't keep your mouth shut long enough to be mysterious."

My heart's beating so fast that I can't find words.

I kind of figured Sasha hated me for lying, for the bet. I know she said she was falling in love with me in the article, but—could Sam and Wade be right? Could she really still have feelings for me? That thought makes my head spin. I want it to be true so badly.

Bobbi adds, "It's going to be all right. You're all going to put on a spectacular performance tonight, and *that* will give people something to talk about. Okay?"

I nod. We all do.

Almost like yes, we're nervous, but not entirely in a bad way. Like the butterflies in our stomachs are just signs of something great to come. I want to reach out to Sasha and tell her about it, that I finally feel like I might belong.

But right now my focus has to be on the music. I'll figure out a way to deal with my feelings for her later.

An assistant knocks on the door to the green room, and after Bobbi lets them in, they tell us, "Five minutes."

Bobbi beams. "It's go time."

28

Sasha

Okay.

Okay.

Okay. I can do this.

I'm backstage at *The Late Late Show,* with a card around my neck that reads *PRESS,* and Claire's pep talk is still fresh in my mind. I'm not sure how Vanessa got me the press card to *The Late Late Show* on such short notice, but I suspect Lloyd may not be aware of this.

That's a problem for later. Now I need to get over my fears and just do this.

Once I'm actually in the studio, most people run past me like I'm invisible. I see assistants being yelled at, probably unfairly, and producers running around backstage. I think I catch a glimpse of an HBO star going to a green room, but before I can waste any time being starstruck, I hear it . . . Penny's voice.

Somewhere nearby, she yells, "One, two, three. . . . Let's go!"

Guitar and bass explode into the silence, followed a second later by the drums. They're so in sync that it takes me aback. I'm stunned, walking slowly toward the stage like I've been hypnotized. They sound better than they ever did, even better than they were at the pop-up concert. Penny's voice booms over the other instruments. Then the solos come, and each one has their chance to shine.

They're finally a band.

Suddenly a woman with large shoulders emerges in front of me. "Press isn't allowed back here." She stares at the card around my neck. "Shouldn't you be in the audience?"

A nervous giggle escapes me, and she gives me a hard look.

"I—actually—"

She narrows her eyes at me. "You're not really with the press, are you? You're too young."

"No, I am!" I bring my card up. "I'm with LA Now."

"Never heard of them." She crosses her arms over her chest, suspicious.

Behind her, a few feet away, I can see the lights coming from the stage. Daniel is a few feet away from me. I can't stop now. Not after coming so far.

I take the card from around my neck and hand it to her. "See for yourself. It's legit."

As she brings it closer to her face for inspection, I take off.

Sadly, I don't manage to make it more than two steps before she throws the card up and catches me in midair. I thrash around, but she has me secured over her shoulders. She radios someone and says, "This is Pauline. We have a boy-band stalker here."

I scowl, facing ahead. "They're not a boy band, actually. They're a *rock* band."

"I'm forty-seven. KISS is a rock band," she quips.

I cock an eyebrow. "Clearly you don't know your genres. KISS may have been rock, but they leaned toward heavy and glam metal."

"Girl, are you going to argue with me right now?" Pauline asks.

She makes it sound like that might not be a very good idea. Her tone of voice plus the fact that I'm still thrown over her shoulders like a sack of potatoes is enough to convince me, so I don't say anything else.

It takes *forever* for two more security goons to come expel me. By that time, the band is already finished with their performance, and Penny is done handling the interview on the couch, though I could barely hear any of it. Pauline hands me over to the guards. On the way out of the studio, I try to make my case.

"I know how this sounds, but I swear I'm not a stalker," I tell the two big men. "I'm friends with the band!"

"Sounds like you're not a very good friend," one of the goons says. The other one laughs, and I glare at them both. In fairness, though, I'm not even sure *I* would believe me.

They only exchange a look and, as we reach the back door, ask me to leave.

Okay, so plan A wasn't very well thought out.

Time for plan B.

It takes twenty-three minutes. Twenty-three minutes for the first van to arrive, but after the first one shows up, the others come as well. At thirty minutes, there are five vans with reporters from various tabloids spread outside the venue.

A few black cars park outside too, surely for the high-profile celebrities who were on the show today, but I'm only interested in one, so I stick as close as I can to the music journalists. I miss my press card, but I've been around the people at LA Now for long enough now that I know that if you *look* like you know what you're doing, people are happy to assume that you do and completely ignore you.

Right now, I'm very happy to be ignored.

Penny leaves first, deep in conversation with Wade. I'm far enough away that they can't see me, but I can see them just fine. They stop to say hello to the reporters, the cameras in their faces as they wave hello and say a few things here and there. I don't catch any of it. My eyes are glued to the exit, and my heart is beating too fast, too hard.

I feel like I might pass out.

And then here he comes . . . Daniel, with Sam by his side.

"Daniel!" I yell.

I'm suddenly acutely aware of how many people are here, all turning to look at me when I scream his name. There must be around fifty, reporters and assistants and drivers and security people. Nobody knows who Daniel is, but it's generally frowned upon to yell any name outside a venue like this.

It's very much . . . intense fan behavior.

All eyes are on me, except for the one person whose attention I need to get.

I take a very deep breath and yell louder this time. "Rotten!"

Now everyone knows who I'm here for. No take-backs.

He raises his head with a frown, but if he sees me, he's not coming my way.

Oh God. Someone is directing him to a car. People in black suits are shielding each of the band members. I have to find anyone with a microphone, and the TMZ van is the closest. I can't come this far only to fail.

I can't let that happen. I *can't.*

I take off running, but this time I run away from him, darting toward one of the TMZ reporters instead. The poor blond woman with a high bun looks confused when I grab her cordless microphone. "I'm so sorry," I whisper to her. "I'll give this back to you."

"Yeah, *now.* Give it back now," she demands.

But I'm on a mission, so I ignore her.

I run to the other side of the van so she can't get me, and

at the top of my lungs, I start singing, "You're just too good to be true . . ."

I don't stop there. I have done my homework. I have watched *10 Things I Hate About You* fifty times now. I can sing this whole song by heart after bawling my eyes out in every scene, even the ones that probably weren't meant to make me cry.

I'm about to serenade the hell out of this boy.

Both the blond reporter and a short man from TMZ try to get me to stop, but I only sing more loudly. I sing at the top of my lungs, so loudly and breathlessly that I'm not sure it's coming out as anything but noise, but I'm doing my best. And judging by the way the other reporters are reacting . . . my best isn't taking me to *Making Music!* anytime soon.

A lot of them have their cameras pointed toward me, but some of them are recording this on their phones. Most of them are laughing. The blond woman finally stops in front of me, one hand covering her ear, the other gesturing at me to stop.

"Keep the microphone. Just—stop singing."

Oops.

As for Daniel, he's just staring at me. His eyes are big, and his brows are furrowed slightly as he takes all this in. I'm afraid to know what he's thinking. Actually, I'm dying to know what he's thinking.

"Daniel, I—I am so sorry. I am sorry about everything. I screwed up, and—" I pause to breathe. The reporters around us press in closer. So rude. "This is the most embarrassing moment of my life. But if I don't die of embarrassment, please forgive me?" I look at him. "I know what I did was bad. But give me a chance to make this up to you. You *were* too good to be true, and I didn't trust it, but I fell so hard for you. I . . . I love you."

My whole body is burning with embarrassment and adrenaline.

Like the Red Sea, the crowd has opened for us.

Daniel stands right in front of me.

29

Daniel

I stop in front of her, my Converse All Stars halting abruptly on the pavement. Our eyes connect, and I swear the only thing I hear is both our heartbeats, loud enough that they echo in this parking lot.

Maybe it's the adrenaline from having performed on *The Late Late Show.* Maybe it's the feeling that the band isn't in any danger anymore, after we killed our performance. Maybe it's knowing that I belong now, that I don't have to exist in the margins of my own dreams. Maybe it's the girl of my dreams running from reporters and singing wildly out of tune that she loves me and wants me back.

Sasha lowers the microphone.

"I'm in love with you, Daniel," she repeats, this time just for me.

My heart might explode. My head might too. The way she says it sounds like *Let's start again.*

"I'm really sorry I wasn't fully honest with you," she says.

"Maybe that's unforgivable, but I needed to tell you how I feel. I need to—"

"Try me."

She stops, blinking. I want to take her in my arms.

But I don't. I wait.

She clears her throat. "Can you forgive me?"

I can't really take it anymore.

I pull her close by her waist and press my lips to hers.

She wraps her arms around my neck, dropping the microphone to the ground. A reporter swears, probably the one who owns the mic, but we don't break the kiss.

In true rom-com fashion, I hold her close and spin her around.

Her eyes widen. "Don't you dare drop me."

I smile. "Don't worry. I got you." And I kiss her again.

The crowd cheers.

In my head, the credits roll.

30

Sasha

ONE YEAR LATER

The second the song ends, I turn down the volume on the radio and look at my boyfriend. Daniel gives me a look, like he's self-conscious, but I roll my eyes, reaching for him across the passenger seat of his car to give him a peck.

"Don't make that face. You guys sound amazing!"

He scratches the back of his head. "You think so?"

He's being humble. Their new single has been on the top of the Billboard chart for a few weeks now, and there's no way you can tune in to a rock station without hearing it. It's such a *him* thing, to convince his band to record a rock version of a classic rom-com song. While their debut album didn't win any awards, it got nominated for seven, and I'm confident the album they're recording now will win *all* the awards. I've been getting sneak peeks, especially of the songs Daniel has written, and it's so raw and honest. I think it'll be my favorite album of all time.

"I *especially* love this song," I say. And it isn't because it's the song I sang off-key and managed to win him back with after their appearance on *The Late Late Show* last summer. It is, objectively, a very good song, and even better with their band covering it.

"I especially love you," he says, cocking an eyebrow, like that's a counter-argument.

I laugh, reaching for his hand.

It's the only thing that stops the fidgety feeling in my stomach. We watch people come and go outside, but we stay in his car, in our world, where nothing can really disrupt us. Except . . .

"You're going to do fine," Daniel offers.

I close my eyes. "If we don't talk about this, it's not happening."

He chuckles, bringing the back of my hand to his lips, and pressing a kiss to it. His mouth is warm, and the brush of his lips sends a shiver up my spine.

"You have to go in, like, a minute," he says.

"No, I don't." I do, actually.

Daniel is far more patient than I could ever be. He says my name sweetly, and when I finally look at him, he asks me, "What has my sister told you about this?"

I take a deep breath and remember Helena's pep talk from two weeks ago. "That I shouldn't be afraid of living my dream." I give this some thought. "And UCLA *is* my dream. Majoring in journalism *is* my dream. But it's . . ."

"Hmm?" He raises his eyebrows.

God, he's gorgeous. It's so distracting. It's infuriating.

"I'm kind of afraid I may not have earned it. I'm only here with this scholarship because of what I wrote about you last summer." I shrug, feeling a little weird.

Daniel shakes his head. "Nonsense. That exposé was worthy of the pages of *Rolling Stone*."

"I hate the word *exposé*," I note.

He ignores me. "You're going to write so much. Nobody will even remember me in a few years, but you're going to have a long and healthy career."

I laugh at that, shaking my head. He always gets me to laugh.

I untangle my hand from his, so I can hold his face and guide him to me. I kiss his cheek, then his other cheek, and when he's watching me very closely, I kiss his mouth. A peck, at first, then an actual kiss.

His hands slide down my shoulders, then up again. He plays with the strap of my dress. . . . Then, very suddenly, he stops kissing me, putting some distance between us with both hands up. "Sasha. You're going to be late for your first day of university. Stop stalling!"

I laugh again, nodding slowly. "Okay, okay. Thank you." I take a deep breath. "For the ride and for giving me the courage. For everything." I open the door. Before I leave, I tell him, "Love you."

"Love you too. Have a good class!" Daniel blows me a

kiss, and I pretend to catch it. It's ridiculously romantic. We have become the type of couple I always rolled my eyes at, and it's the best.

In the car, Daniel puts his sunglasses back on, turns on the radio, and drives off with a big smile.

I turn to the UCLA campus, ready to meet Claire on our first day together. My heart is still warm.

I'm ready.

Acknowledgments

Muito obrigada em primeiro lugar à Mamis, minha primeira fã, que sempre acredita em todas as minhas ideias e vê só o bom em tudo o que eu faço. Nada como o teu amor pra me motivar a me manter no caminho que, com teu apoio, eu mesma escolhi.

Thank you to my spectacular agent, Chelsea Eberly, a partner in this wild business who, in spite of the very unpredictable nature of publishing, always makes me feel safe. Thank you to my editor, Hannah Hill, who made this book infinitely better with her passion for romantic comedies and her understanding of the characters and what they and the story needed. Thank you to cover designer Casey Moses and illustrator Flor Fuertes, who together brought the magic of 2000s rom-com movie posters to this beautiful cover, capturing the exact feel of what the book is at its core. To the Delacorte/Underlined team, thank you so much for all your hard work and inspiration.

My dear friends, Alyssa, Robin, Natasha, Louisa, Joelle, Aayushi, Vanshika, Elisa, Sofia, Ams, Priyanka, Mith, Joana, Adriano, Camila, Luma, Isa, and Ananya. Your support is surreal and makes my heart warm. I hope you never get tired of me and my ramblings. Your friendship and hand-holding mean the world to me.

Thank you to all the lovely people who supported my debut last year with *Like a Love Song* and made sure the start of my journey was as beautiful as could be: Lou—especially you, always you—Laura, Adri, Carmen, Skye, CW, Cande, Aishwarya, Nina, Jennifer, Casey, Erick, Sil, Sonora, Ycel, Cossette, Lily, Paola, Hanna, Brittany, Soumi, Cam, Lili, Emery, Anna, Ameet, Lauren, Alexander, Maya, Chai, and Allie.

A major thank-you to the people who bring books to the hands of teens: librarians, booksellers, teachers, and bloggers. I cannot thank you enough. You have authors' backs, and for that we'll be forever grateful.

Finally, to my former students, every single one of them. Thank you. Titier ama vocês bbs.

About the Author

GABRIELA MARTINS is a Brazilian kidlit author and linguist. Her stories feature Brazilian characters finding themselves and love. She was a high school teacher and has also worked as a TED-Ed Club facilitator, where she helped teens develop their own talks in TED format. She edited and self-published a pro-bono LGBTQ+ anthology (*Keep Faith*) with all funds going to queer people in need. When she's not writing, she can be found cuddling with her two cats or singing loudly and off-key. Gabriela is the author of *Like a Love Song* and *Bad at Love.*

gabrielawrites.com